Published by Audrey Harrison

© Copyright 2020 Audrey Harrison

Find more about the author and contact details at the end of this book and the chance to obtain a free copy of The Unwilling Earl.

Chapter 1

Dear Lord Longdon,

Please forgive my writing to you, but I do not feel there is anyone else I can express my concerns to.

You see, I think I'm being followed.

Your sister told me everything about what happened with Mr. Sage and Mr. Malone. As her best friend, I can assure you of my silence with regard to the details. I am just so relieved that she is no longer in danger from Mr. Sage and that no forced elopement took place.

I would normally write to Edith about my concerns, but she is on her wedding trip, and I cannot in all conscience disrupt that. I would not normally have contacted you, only I genuinely feel my safety is at risk. Please be assured that I am not one prone to dramatics or hysterics; in fact, I pride myself on being completely the opposite.

For the last sennight, I have noticed that whenever I have stepped outside there has been a man in the shadows near my home. I did not recognise him at first; he is very unkempt and dishevelled. One night, though, I foolishly approached him and asked him what he wanted. I was accompanied by a servant, so was not taking too much of a risk, but I felt great alarm when I realised who it was: Mr. Malone.

He asked if I could spare some pennies, and I admit I gave him all that I had in my reticule – recognising him had shaken me so much. He acted as if we had never met before, until I was walking away and he muttered, "I'll see you again soon. Very soon."

His words, I confess, unsettled me, and although I have ensured that a male servant is with me whenever I leave home, he is still there. All of the time.

I am afraid and embarrassed to admit that if I confessed any of my concerns to my stepmother, she would not take them seriously. My father is very much influenced by her, so there is no point seeking assistance from them. The only other family I have at home is my half-brother, and he is still in the schoolroom, so you see my dilemma? I hope you understand, for I feel unsafe and cannot think of anyone else to turn to for assistance.

I can only think that my fortune is his motivation for targeting me. To what end, whether it is purely to obtain money from me in larger amounts, I do not know. I cannot quite allow myself to dwell on any other reason, but it does niggle at the back of my mind. Why he is no longer in society I presume has to do with what happened to Edith, but, believe me, he looks as if he has fallen on very hard times; strange, when it was only weeks ago that he was in the finest ballrooms in London. I would have supposed he had the funds to set up somewhere away from your family.

If you could offer me advice as to what to do, I would be most grateful. I admit to being a little perturbed and unsure of the best course of action to take. I would hate to make an unnecessary fuss, but I am concerned.

Your friend,
Susan King

There. It was done. Only fear for her safety had pushed her to contact the man she loved, who barely knew of her existence. She could only hope that he would offer some guidance or help, for she wasn't being overly dramatic in expressing that she had no one else to ask for assistance.

She had never felt so alone and vulnerable in her life, and she was in the middle of the busiest city in the world.

*

"Susan, you can be the most annoying chit a woman ever had the misfortune to be related to," scolded Mrs. King, Susan's stepmother. "Will you at least try to look your best when you're attending one of the biggest functions of the season?"

"But peach makes me look sickly," Susan protested feebly. Their encounters were always the same, even after fifteen years of being related. Susan was the despised stepdaughter, the darling of her father, and a woman who, if the scolding by her stepmother was to be believed, was intent on putting off every possible suitor the season had to offer.

"Mr. Lawson said he liked peach. Therefore, you will wear peach for his ball," Mrs. King responded as the modistes hovered in the background, glancing at each other in discomfort.

"As I don't wish to give Mr. Lawson the slightest indication that I might be willing to accept any proposal he'd be foolish enough to offer, I would prefer to wear a different colour," Susan said, setting her shoulders. "Please get me some options of pale blue," she said to the head modiste. For once feeling as if she was in control of some part of her life, if only a little.

5

The women bustled to the piles of fabric they'd brought with them to the large house on Curzon Street, leaving stepmother and stepdaughter alone for a few moments.

Mrs. King approached Susan and, before there was time to react, grabbed the fabric of Susan's simple cotton day dress and dragged the girl to her. "Listen to me, brat," she hissed. "You might be of age, but you are marrying this season; do I make myself clear? I am sick to death of seeing your ugly face in my home. I've reached my limit. You will accept someone in the next month, or I will arrange a marriage for you. Your father will agree with me, obviously, so don't go whining to him. We're sick of seeing your pained expressions every day. It's time you married."

Susan swallowed. She had been browbeaten for the last fifteen years, and it was hard to stand up to after such a long period of time. Only the desire to marry a man she loved gave her some of the inner strength she needed to face her tormentor.

"As I am of age, I can't be forced into marriage."

"Oh, can you not? I'm sure I can contrive to arrange a little situation in which I would shout out loud and clear that you had been compromised. A sure way to get you to the altar whatever your feelings on the matter."

"You wouldn't!"

"Test me, and we'll see you married by the end of the week," came the snarling promise.

A quiet cough alerted them that the modiste wished to approach them. Mrs. King stood back. "Have whatever dress you like – just make sure the neckline is plunging. You have one asset; at least you can show that part of you off," Mrs. King instructed before sweeping out of the room.

6

Susan's cheeks burned, not helped by the looks of sympathy she was receiving from the women who were fussing around her in an effort to appear normal.

"Do you have my measurements?" Susan asked after a few moments of being treated with care and consideration, which had made her feel even more oppressed.

"Yes, miss."

"In that case, I shall have those two designs, this in the blue and the second in the white. Please make the bodices a respectable height," Susan said with a blush.

"Of course."

"Please excuse me, but I think I've no need to delay you any longer. Thank you for your time," Susan said, walking out of the room.

She entered her bedchamber and leaned on the closed door. She couldn't take much more of the abuse, the undermining, and now the promise of ruination. There was no doubt her mother would carry out her threat, and it horrified Susan.

She was an heiress, true, but she wasn't beautiful. Looks didn't necessarily matter if one had an inheritance. A girl with a fortune could always guarantee a husband, whether she be plain or pretty. If she liked that husband was another matter.

Susan moved over to the cheval mirror that stood in the corner, always a reminder that she hadn't inherited her mother's beauty, just her height and large bosom. The first Mrs. King had been stunning to look at: tumbling golden locks and clear blue eyes to enhance a tall, shapely figure.

Susan was three and twenty and had light brown hair and blue-green eyes. It was as if when she was being created, no one could decide what she should have, so they

7

gave her everything. Hair that turned lighter in summer, but not light enough to be classed as blonde, and darker in winter, though not dark enough to be an interesting brunette. Her lips were a little too full, and her nose didn't have the aquiline shape the aristocracy preferred. All in all, she could barely be classed as pretty, very often attracting the label of unremarkable, or the even more damning compliment of being personable. Added to which, she had been cruelly given the epithet of "Plain Jane", by her stepmother, meaning her confidence about her looks was about as low as it could be.

She was of a quiet nature, partly forced by the fact that every time she spoke, her stepmother contradicted her. It was easier to remain silent than to face constant belittlement. Now, after years of being suppressed, she sometimes wondered who the real Susan King was, for she could barely remember herself.

Mr. King indulged his daughter, but only when they were alone. He had remarried for looks, not personality, and now when his second wife's looks had faded, there was little else to recommend her. He was a malleable man who bowed to his chosen one's wishes, even if they were to the detriment of his daughter. He found it made his life easier, and he could ease his conscience by delighting in spoiling his daughter when they were alone.

Feeling confined by her home situation, added to which was the apprehension of daily conflict, now heightened by the certainty she was being followed, Susan longed for relief. Making a decision, she grabbed a straw bonnet off her wardrobe shelf and went down the servants' stairs to the kitchens.

It was a route she had used often, both in their London home and in the country house in Warwickshire. It was her way of escaping from her stepmother's all-seeing eyes. The staff knew full well how Mrs. King treated her stepdaughter and unobtrusively did all they could to support and cosset the gentle young girl.

Entering the kitchen, she was greeted by Cook. "Now then, missy, what are you doing here? Thought you were picking out frocks to dazzle all them fine gentlemen with."

Grimacing, Susan picked up a shortbread biscuit, always available in the kitchen. "Mother wanted plunging necklines and colours that would make me look like some sort of sickly Gothic heroine," she said, sitting on a stool. "I had to escape."

Cook clicked her tongue in disapproval but said nothing. She would rant to the housekeeper later, but it was best to hold her counsel for now. "And what does sneaking down here and eating biscuits do to help? You'll be getting thickset, like me, and your dancing days will be over. You should hold me up as a warning."

Susan grinned. "You shouldn't make biscuits that taste so good; then I wouldn't eat so many. I'm actually going to have a walk around the garden after I've finished this."

"Not going to Hyde Park?"

"No." Susan frowned. "I think I'll just remain within our grounds for today." She felt unable to appear confident if she were to see Mr. Malone, after the tongue-lashing her stepmother had given her. She needed a little time to regain her equilibrium, which she had to do most days.

"I'll have a nice bit of ice cream for you when you've finished your stroll," Cook promised.

"Mm, you make ice cream almost as well as you make biscuits." Susan smiled, moving from the chair.

Popping her bonnet on her head, she left the kitchen, and after passing the scullery and cold store, she emerged into the small kitchen garden. A gate in the wall led to the formal part of the grounds, which wasn't huge in comparison to those found on country estates, but large enough for a reasonable walk if she didn't mind doubling back over some of the pathways.

Susan decided to pick some of the flowers from the overflowing beds to brighten up her bedchamber. On hearing a creak behind her, she paused. She turned slowly, letting out a whoosh of breath when she saw nothing. She was clearly alone.

Cursing herself for hearing threats that weren't there, she continued in her task. Her thoughts drifted to Lord Longdon who would have received her letter by now. Writing to him had been folly; she had been desperate for help, and he was the only person she could seek advice from, but she knew her inner feelings had driven her as well. She had been in love with him for years, before he'd even gone to fight with Wellington in the Peninsular War. She thought he'd return after Napoleon had been defeated, but no, he'd gone to America to fight there, and then had followed Wellington to France.

She'd seen a difference in him when the fighting had finally ended. It was no surprise really – he'd been fighting for years; one couldn't be unaffected by that – but her feelings hadn't changed. Not one bit. A pity he hardly seemed to notice her other than as the best friend of his sister.

She was destined to admire from afar, and although she'd never expected to actually marry him, there had always been a flicker of hope while they both remained single. Now, thanks to her stepmother, even that was about

10

to be permanently extinguished. For there was one thing that was certain about the second Mrs. King: once she decreed something had to happen, it occurred within a surprisingly short amount of time. She'd decided Susan was to marry, and without a doubt that would happen, whether Susan wished it or not.

Sighing, she turned and stopped walking suddenly, her mouth dropping open in a silent 'o'.

"Don't make a sound and you won't get hurt," Mr. Malone said, pointing a gun in her direction.

Susan faltered, staring at the weapon pointing at her. Her heart pounded noisily, and her breathing was shallow. Afraid she was going to faint at the sight of the glinting silver aimed at her, she took a steadying breath. Panicking would not help her, so there was no point in wasting her energy on it.

"I can give you money, but I haven't any on my person at the moment," Susan said, surprised that her voice, although shaky, was clear.

"I don't want the pennies you'd throw at me," he sneered. "It's you I'm here for. You're coming with me."

"What? No!" Susan wanted to run, but she could see the gun was primed. "I can give you more than I did last time."

"Yes, you can, but not in the way you think," Albert Malone answered. "Stop trying to delay. Come with me, or your father will be mourning the loss of his only daughter."

Susan paused. She was terrified, but the oddness of the situation struck her forcibly. "You are trying to kidnap me, but if you shoot me, I'm no use to you at all."

"Just stop talking and come on! You infuriating baggage!" Albert cursed.

"No," Susan said, gaining strength from goodness knew where. "I'm not coming with you."

The crack of the gunshot startled the birds around the garden; there were squawks of complaint as the ruffled creatures took flight.

Susan fell backwards to the hard ground with such force it took her breath away. She gasped, struggling to inhale. Black dots appeared around the edges of her eyes, and her vision started to fade. She could feel herself being roughly handled and heard cursing. The last thing she saw was the rough, dirty face of Albert Malone.

Chapter 2

Miles reread the letter, his stomach churning. Miss King wasn't the type of young lady to create theatrical melodramas; in fact she was a sensible young woman. One who would attract the title of bookish and pleasing, rather than a comment about the beauty of her features. She wasn't overtly attractive, yet Miles had always thought she had something about her that made her a little different from the usual simpering misses one had the misfortune of meeting.

He stood, walked to the bell pull and tugged the rope, waiting impatiently for the almost immediate entry of his butler.

When the door opened, he turned to face his member of staff. "I'm going to London today. I'll be riding ahead, but send instructions to Ashurst that he needs to follow me at speed."

"Yes, m'lud."

Miles frowned as he read through the letter once more. There would only be one reason Albert was targeting his sister's best friend, and that was for her fortune. The only way he would succeed would be to compromise the chit. His blood ran cold at the thought of someone being hurt because he hadn't made sure that Albert had disappeared when their paths had crossed the last time.

Thinking back to when he'd last seen Albert, he scowled. Miles had beaten him senseless for being involved in a plan for his own sister to be kidnapped by a rogue

13

whom Albert had introduced into their circle. Miles had threatened Albert with worse than the beating he'd received if he dared to come into polite society and try the same trick on some other unsuspecting family. Miles had spread the word through his network of military men that Albert was no longer to be trusted. It ensured the man wouldn't receive a welcome in any reputable society. It was a pity, because Albert had been a fine cavalry officer when it had mattered, but a decent officer never betrayed his fellow men, and Albert had done that most spectacularly.

Cursing, Miles ran a hand through his hair; he should have checked that Albert had left London. He had presumed he would. He should have known better. Now, if Miss King's words were true, Albert was desperate, and it was partly Miles's reaction to him that had caused it. That made Albert less likely to be constricted by ethics or morals, which made the intended victim even more vulnerable.

Miles left his study, running up the stairs two at a time. Albert had been in his cavalry regiment when they'd fought abroad in the Peninsular War and at Waterloo. He was a good cavalryman, a cold killer, a soldier who had volunteered and led some of the "forlorn hopes" to gain promotion. As those same forlorn hopes usually had little chance of being successful, the men who volunteered were hardened, or desperate for promotion and reward should they survive. Only the men with nothing to lose volunteered for those missions. Albert had always returned. He was a lethally effective killer, and he was targeting an innocent girl. Miles had to get to her. Fast.

*

14

Arriving in London early that evening, Miles stopped at his town house in Curzon Street to change before approaching the Kings. From the information in the letter, he would have to tread carefully in order to find out from Miss King what the latest news was.

One of the senior footmen helped him to dress in some of the clothes he kept in Curzon Street. His valet would not arrive until the following day at the earliest. Miles chose evening attire, in case he had to chase across London to find the ball or soirée the Kings were attending that evening. He gave his frock-coat a last tug, nodded to the footman and hurried downstairs, impatient to leave.

Stepping onto the marble of the hallway, he turned to another footman. "If my mother should arrive home with her friends before I do, advise her that I have arrived from Barrowfoot House, but I shall only be returning late tonight. I will see her at breakfast, or luncheon tomorrow."

His mother being out was a blessing; she would have delayed him with a thousand questions and then gossiped about what had been happening in town. Better to face her on the morrow when he had concocted a more feasible reason for travelling to London at such speed. He would be more relaxed when he knew that Susan was safe.

The Kings lived only ten doors away from his own home. Something of which his sister, Edith, and Susan had taken full advantage during their stay in London. It had been quite usual to see one or the other coming and going between the two houses without the need for a chaperone. No one would lift an eyebrow at them scurrying along such a short distance.

It seemed that light blazed from each window of the Kings' abode. With increasing trepidation, Miles knocked on the door and waited.

A flustered servant opened the door. "I'm sorry, sir, the family are not receiving calls at this time."

"I need to speak to Miss King. If you tell her Lord Longdon has arrived, I'm sure she'll see me," Miles responded.

The servant paled.

"What has happened? Am I too late?" Miles demanded.

"I— the family— Miss King …" came the stuttered response.

"For goodness' sake, stand aside, man!" Miles said, walking into the entrance of the house. "Either take me to Miss King or her father."

"Yes, m'lord."

Miles was taken to the study of Mr. King. Barely waiting until he'd been announced, he entered the room as soon as begrudging compliance was heard from the gentleman inside the study.

"My lord, please excuse us. We are not ourselves this evening," Mr. King said, standing to greet his unexpected guest.

"I gather not. Forgive my abruptness, but where is your daughter?" There was no point being constrained by the niceties of etiquette.

Mr. King sat heavily in his chair. "You have heard something? If that is the case, it is worse than we thought."

Mrs. King had been seated when Miles had entered the study. She'd nodded to Miles but had offered no greeting. At Mr. King's reaction she turned to her husband. "Of course it's going to get out. The child has ruined herself

16

and us in the process. How is Stuart going to be able to attend a decent college with her shame fuelling the gossip columns for goodness knows how long?" she snapped.

"Please," Mr. King pleaded, his head in his hands. "Not now, my dear. Not now."

"If I could interrupt?" Miles asked, moving towards Mr. King and ignoring the outburst from Mrs. King. "Where is your daughter?"

Mr. King seemed to age before Miles's eyes. "She's gone. We don't know where, or even if she's dead or alive."

Miles stilled. "What do you mean? Tell me all you know." His tone brokered no argument, immediately in charge. On the inside he was trying to suppress an unexpected surge of panic.

"She was out in the garden this morning. The servants heard a loud noise but didn't think anything of it at first. It was only when one of the maids went to look for my daughter at my wife's request that the evidence was found," Mr. King said dully.

"And the evidence was?" Miles asked through gritted teeth. Precious time was being wasted. He could have shaken Mr. King in frustration, but he held his patience.

"There was a discarded bunch of flowers. My daughter often picked them for her room, or my study." Mr. King smiled and then hesitated, his colour fading even further. "And there was a bloodstain on the ground. They now think that what they heard was a gunshot," he choked out.

"Sir, your daughter wrote to me a letter, which I received today. She expressed some concern about a gentleman we all know, Albert Malone. I know him more particularly because he served with me as one of my cavalrymen. I managed to foil a plot he was intent on

17

carrying out against my own sister, and I had presumed he'd left the country. It seems your daughter has seen him loitering around this address in recent days, and he appeared in dire straits," Miles explained quickly.

"She never mentioned any of it," Mr. King said.

"Probably not wishing to cause worry, or undue concern," Miles said in defence of Susan, not revealing what she'd confessed about her family in her letter. Although in his mind they were far worse than how Susan had described. "I'm presuming something has happened involving Malone. I don't think the two occurrences are a coincidence."

"She could have eloped with him," Mrs. King said.

"Why would she do that?" Mr. King for once snapped at his wife. "If she wanted to marry someone, she knew how much you would welcome the news. There would be no need for her to elope with anyone. I would have accepted anyone she chose."

"She is three and twenty, well beyond the age of marrying. Perhaps she managed to persuade some fool to take her on," Mrs. King bit back.

"She hasn't eloped. That's a nonsensical suggestion," Miles said, with little regard to how his words would be received. "There would be no sign of a struggle if she had. What have you done to recover her, sir? I've no need to point out that time is of the essence." He was burning with anger at a woman who should have cared for her stepdaughter. It wasn't as if Susan was an unpleasant girl, she was everything pleasing and warm. A pity her family didn't seem to realise her value, Miles thought angrily.

"I've instructed the Bow Street Runners to search for her. They are looking in the city, but there are two on their way to Gretna Green, in case she has been taken there," Mr. King said.

"Good. I will do my own search, if that is agreeable to you. I know men who might know more about Malone's movements in the city, and maybe we can find out if his friend has returned. We know his accomplice left the shores for the Continent," Miles explained. Charles Sage had been barely conscious when he'd been carried aboard the ship he'd hired to elope with Miles's sister, Edith. Her future husband had given him a beating he was hardly likely to forget.

"I will gladly accept any help you can give, my lord," Mr. King said.

"It seems that your family's actions have caused my stepdaughter's disappearance," Mrs. King said, indignant.

"And it seems your behaviour prevented Miss King from seeking help from the people who should have protected her the most," Miles replied.

"How dare you!" Mrs. King spluttered.

"I dare because a young girl is goodness knows where, with a man intent on gaining her fortune in whatever way he can," Miles said. "She is injured, to what extent we don't know, and you, madam, couldn't give a fig as to her welfare."

Mr. King let out a sob, and Miles left the room. He blamed both parents for their neglect of Susan. If she'd been able to turn to them, she would have been better protected from the moment she'd noticed Albert Malone. Her parents weren't wholly responsible, though; some of the situation was down to his own folly. He should have checked to ensure that Albert had left London when Edith was threatened.

Leaving the house, he turned towards Hyde Park. It was time to visit his old barracks.

19

*

Entering Hyde Park Barracks always felt like coming home to Miles. Some of the men who billeted there were like brothers to him, all having shared common experiences, bonding them together in a way the general populace wouldn't and couldn't understand.

In the officer's mess, he was relieved to find two of his most trusted friends. Both were captains alongside himself, and all had served in the three main land conflicts Britain had been involved with in recent years.

"Jones! Dunn! Am I glad to see you two!" Miles approached the pair, who were seated, boots resting on a low table, each enjoying a glass of amber liquid.

"What's to do, Longdon?" Jones drawled, taking a long draw of one of the cigars they all liked to smoke since their return from the Peninsula.

"Have either of you seen or heard anything from Malone? Or about him?" Miles asked, leaning on one of the empty chairs. Now was not the time to sit and chat.

"Not since you gave him a good beating and told us what the blaggard tried to do," Dunn responded. "Is he still hanging around? Thought he'd go to ground for a time."

"So did I. I told him in no uncertain terms to do so," Miles said. "Unfortunately, the dog seems to have abducted my sister's friend. There is the possibility of a gunshot wound, for there is a patch of blood where she was last known to be. We don't know how badly she might be injured, so it's important I find him, or anything I can about him and where he might have taken her."

"By Gad! That goes beyond the pale!" Jones exclaimed, sitting up. "That's not good *ton*. Shooting at young girls? Good God, whatever next?"

20

Miles had to suppress a smile. Jones and Dunn were both younger sons, as he had been when he'd joined the cavalry. The sudden death of his father and then, in the following two years, his two elder brothers had seen Miles thrust unexpectedly into the position of head of the family, with all its responsibilities. Only after Waterloo had he resigned his commission, but his friends were still very much a part of the cavalry.

The three had seen each other through all sorts of scrapes, and the bond held firm now the fighting was done. Miles was dark, but Dunn and Jones were both blonde. He used to call them his protective angels, for they both had cherubic faces, although Dunn's now held the scar of a badly aimed bayonet. Jones was usually quite uninterested in others' situations, more inclined to utter a witty remark than take offence. His agitation about Susan's disappearance likely reflected only the slightest hint of the anger he was feeling.

"They were intent on taking my sister to Scotland by boat, so I'm heading to the docks to see if I can find anything out there. Bow Street Runners are travelling on the North Road towards Gretna, so that side of things is covered. Can you try to find out what you can from Albert's cronies?" Miles asked.

Jones stood quickly. "Of course."

"I'll come with you, Longdon," Dunn said. "You'll have a lot of ground to cover on your own."

"Thank you. Shall we convene back here in two hours?" Miles asked.

The two men nodded, and they each went on their tasks. Miles was relieved he had their support. There was a lot to do, and every moment counted. He only hoped Susan had the fortitude to face whatever she had to before they rescued her. For he was determined they were going to.

Chapter 3

Albert paced the cabin. "There's no sign of improvement?" he snapped.

Charles Sage moved from the side of the bed. "No. She's still feverish. Why you had to shoot her, you fool, I'll never understand. She's our ticket to comfort. If she dies, we're out of ideas and running from the hangman for the rest of our lives!"

"No one will link her disappearance to us," Albert said, finally ceasing to stride across the small space and sitting on a wooden chair beside a table.

"Oh, will they not?" Charles sneered. "You don't think that captain friend of yours won't link the failed abduction of his sister to the disappearance of her friend? I wonder at your intelligence if you don't think he'll be soon on our tail."

Albert rubbed his hand through his hair. "He's out of town. It will all be over by the time he hears. The deed will be done."

"I hope you're right, because we are out of options if you're not."

"We could just send a kidnap message, asking for a ransom for her release. That would end this sooner, and we won't have to continue playing nursemaids," Albert said, perking up a little at his idea.

"No. We want access to all of her income. Five thousand a year will do us just fine. Why should we settle for less?" Charles replied. "And it will help to make up for being stuck on this damned ship for the weeks I've had to hide out."

The barque was a small ship for its class. Run by a captain and crew who didn't ask any questions about the cargo, dead or alive, that they were transporting. Albert and Charles had paid a substantial amount to enable them to occupy what would have normally been the captain's cabin. It was a large room, but sparsely furnished, just a table, chairs, a bed that was also used as a long seat during the day, as there wasn't enough room for both, a wardrobe, and a washstand behind a screen.

Albert and Charles slept in the cabin next to the captain's so they could be on hand if their captive woke, and so they could make sure no one else had access to their cargo. They were under no illusion that an innocent woman wouldn't be a temptation for most of the depraved sailors on board. It meant the two men were never fully relaxed, and their nerves were beginning to fray from the constant strain they were under.

Albert walked over to where Susan lay, unconscious and fevered, on the bed. "Rather you than me being married to this one. I don't know if I could wake up to her every morning for the rest of my days."

"A good thing you won't have to then," Charles said. "Her inheritance is plentiful enough to help me put up with most things."

"Don't forget my portion."

"I won't. You will be living in luxury with us and have a healthy allowance," Charles assured him. "We're in this together. I haven't forgotten that."

"As long as you do remember," Albert muttered. "I'm going on deck. Never could stand to be in the sick room." He moved to the door and opened it. "Billy! Come and do your nursing!"

A young boy entered the room and walked immediately to the bed. He was dressed in sailor's attire, but the clothing looked as though it had belonged to a larger sailor before being handed down to the boy. He was dark haired, and his skin was already weathered, but he had a kind face and approached Susan concern in his expression. Looking at Susan and feeling her forehead, he tsked. "Have you not been cooling her?" he asked.

"No, that's your job," Albert said as he walked through the door.

"I'm relying on you to keep her alive," Charles said to the young boy. "We have a few days before we arrive in Scotland. I'm expecting her to be well by then."

"Even if the fever breaks, she won't be able to go anywhere for a time. She'll take a while to recover," Billy pointed out.

"Then I'll carry her." Charles left the cabin to follow his friend.

Billy busied himself by fetching fresh water and sponging Susan's hot forehead and cheeks. "It'll be best for you if you don't wake up, missy," he said quietly. "But I daren't risk them finding out if I neglect you. That's more than my life's worth, but what awaits you I wouldn't wish on anyone, especially not a fine young lady. Best if you remain asleep."

*

Albert and Charles checked on Susan regularly but never seemed to show any inclination to stay with her for more than a few minutes. Billy had sole care of her, and although his knowledge was limited, he tried to keep her comfortable. He could see that she was improving, but his sympathy over what she would suffer when she awoke kept him reporting that there was no change in her condition. It was a risk to himself if he were found out, but he couldn't do much to help her, so he did the little he could.

As he watched over her on their second day, Susan moaned. Billy rushed to her side. "Shh, miss. You don't want to make any loud noises."

Susan frowned. She hadn't heard that voice before. She felt very strange. She was moving but she couldn't tell how. Perhaps she was in a carriage, but she couldn't hear the sound of horses' hooves, or the trundling of the wheels. There were few sounds to focus on, apart from an unusual creaking that she couldn't place. She tried to move, but a pain shot through her arm and she moaned again.

"Oh, please be quiet," she heard a pleading voice say.

It sounded afraid, and she responded to that. She didn't want to upset whoever she was with. He sounded young, and she didn't want to distress him further. She struggled to open her eyes, but it was a while before her slow, laboured blinks cleared her vision enough to be able to see.

A pale, worried child looked into her eyes. He was only about fifteen, thin and unkempt, but his eyes held nothing but concern. "If they hear you're awake they'll drag you ashore," he whispered urgently. "You need to pretend you're still asleep, especially if someone comes into the cabin."

Susan nodded her understanding, although she felt complete confusion. Ashore? What could he mean? She tried to remember her last memories, before the darkness

26

had set in, but she couldn't. It was a struggle to keep her eyes open, and when thinking became too much, she let her lids close and let the blackness wrap around her once more.

Billy let out the breath he'd been holding when he saw Susan slip back into unconsciousness. He'd been terrified she'd call out, thinking he was her enemy, which would have resulted in her real enemies being alerted to her recovery.

Leaning back on the chair he was sitting on, he wiped his hands on his breeches, getting rid of the sweat that had developed in his panic. There was very little he could do, but he'd try to protect her in his own way. He'd never seen such a fine lady; her clothes were made of materials of the highest quality, but they had been ruthlessly ripped to reveal the gunshot wound in her shoulder. Her hair was soft, and although it had been tied in curls with ringlets falling around her face, it was now scattered in disarray across her pillow.

Billy's stomach sank. Now she was regaining consciousness, it was only a matter of time before she would be faced with a danger from which no one could save her.

*

It was dark the next time Susan stirred. Her head thudded painfully and she wanted a drink. "Water," she croaked, not knowing if anyone was near.

"Shh," said the same voice as before. "Let me raise you, and you can drink this, but sip it slowly, miss."

Susan did as she was bid, glad for some cool liquid to touch her cracked lips. After too short a time the water was taken away from her and she was laid down gently.

27

"Please keep quiet," the young boy urged.

"I will," Susan said with difficulty. "Where am I?"

"You're on the *Dolphin*, heading to Scotland. You're injured, and it's better that no one knows you've awakened. We'll be arriving at the port tomorrow. The more you can pretend sleep, the better for you," he said quietly, his mouth near Susan's ear.

"Why?" Susan whispered, frowning. "I can't remember why I'm on board a ship. I know that's very stupid of me, for I should know, but I don't seem to be able to remember."

Billy gulped. If he told her, she could become hysterical, but if he remained silent, she might not perceive the danger she was in. "If I tell you everything, will you promise to stay quiet? It's very important."

Susan nodded. "Who are you?"

"Billy, miss. I'm the captain's cabin boy, and I look after anyone who's ill on board, as well as keeping the captain's quarters clean."

"Hello, Billy," Susan said politely.

"Hello, miss," Billy answered. "I'm sorry to upset you, but you were kidnapped by Mr. Malone and Mr. Sage."

A moment or two passed before Susan responded. "I remember. Yes. Mr. Malone. He was following me. I was in the garden at home."

"I don't know about that," Billy said. "I just know there was a big commotion when you came on board. You were shot, you see."

"Oh. Was I?" Susan asked, but Billy wasn't sure she was really taking in his words. "That isn't good. Am I going to die?"

"I don't think so, miss," Billy said with a slight smile in his voice. He'd never spoken to a fine lady before, but he

28

liked this one. "It's your shoulder. They say the bullet went straight through, but you developed a fever."

"Ah. I see," Susan responded thickly. "I'm glad you're looking after me, Billy. I'd like to go to sleep now, if you don't mind. I feel very tired."

"Just remember when you wake not to make a sound," Billy reminded her. He wasn't actually convinced she'd heard him as she slipped back into darkness.

Settling himself on the floor, under a blanket, he thought she would have a peaceful night's sleep. The fever seemed to have broken, which was a relief to some extent. Although he worried about her being discovered awake, he didn't wish any harm on her. She'd spoken very kindly to him. Kinder than anyone ever had as far as he could remember.

*

Albert walked into the cabin. "This is ridiculous! Can we not pour a jug of water over her and wake her?" he demanded of Charles and Billy.

"No, sir," Billy said. "She's not just sleeping; it's deeper than that. It's because of the fever. I'm sure she'll recover soon, but it takes time with females."

"Make yourself scarce, boy," Albert snarled at Billy.

"Yes, sir." Billy gave Susan one last worried glance before he left the room.

"What are we going to do? We can't stay anchored onshore forever, and every moment that passes is a moment we risk discovery," Albert said to Charles.

"You need to relax. True, the signs of the struggle in the garden make it more likely they'll be looking for a kidnapper," Charles said. "But even if they do suspect a dash to the border, whether against her will or not, they'll go heading towards Gretna, and we are on the opposite coastline. She'll be married before they realise their mistake. No one will discover our plans. The only man who could suspect what we're doing is living far from London. It's all under control."

"You'd better be right. I don't want to hang for this," Albert muttered.

"Don't worry. This time all eventualities have been covered," Charles said, crossing to Susan. He lifted the arm that hadn't been hurt and released it. It fell heavily onto the bed; Susan didn't flicker. "Nothing. The boy's speaking the truth. Females are feeble things at the best of times. I'd get used to the idea of being stuck on here for a few more days."

Albert looked as if to say something, but as Billy knocked on the door, he remained quiet.

Walking in with a fresh jug of water, Billy busied himself, not making eye contact with either man. They scared him, but he was used to men who were cruel just for the sake of it. He'd been on this ship for a number of years and had suffered much abuse as a result. The type of sailors who could turn a blind eye to a young woman's kidnap were not the sort to show compassion to anything weaker than themselves. Billy had found they took great pleasure in tormenting and punishing a young boy.

It wasn't long before Albert and Charles left the room with the instruction that if she woke, Billy was to inform them immediately. Billy nodded his acquiescence. He waited until a few minutes had passed before approaching Susan.

"Miss?" he whispered.

"Yes, I'm awake," Susan answered quietly.

"It's safe for the moment. Would you like a drink?"

"Yes, please," Susan answered, opening her eyes. She was more alert this time and looked around the cabin while Billy retrieved a cup from the table.

Lifting Susan gently, he supported her while she drank. This she did thirstily. "Thank you," she murmured when the cup was empty.

"I brought in some bread and jam. It was all I could wrap in my pocket." He brought out a small parcel, wrapped in waxed paper. "Do you think you could eat it?"

"Yes. I'm very hungry. I was afraid my stomach would rumble when they were in the room," Susan admitted.

"Turn onto your side," Billy instructed. "I want you to be able to flop onto your back if anyone should come in."

Susan wriggled around, closing her eyes as a wave of dizziness threatened to overcome her. When it had passed, she gingerly accepted the parcel and started to eat.

Billy stood near the door, listening for footsteps outside the room while Susan ate as quickly as she could. The young boy's nervousness was infectious, although she was trying to remain outwardly calm.

When she'd finished, she indicated she needed another drink, which Billy supplied. Thankful when Susan lay back down, he relaxed a little.

She gingerly touched her wounded arm. "This hurts," she whispered.

"I'm sure it does. I haven't any real bandages, so I had to rip your petticoat. I'm awful sorry," Billy said. It had been the cleanest piece of cloth he had access to.

"It's fine," Susan responded with a smile. "It's very good of you to shield me from those men. You are being very brave."

31

"It ain't right what they're trying to do."

"What are they intending? Do you know?"

"You promise you won't have hysterics?" Billy asked.

Susan smiled. "I'm not an hysterical sort of woman. I promise."

"Mr. Sage is going to marry you, and you're going to live together in a big house. Do you really have five thousand a year?" Billy was unable to keep the wonder out of his voice.

"Yes. Unfortunately, I do," Susan answered.

"You say yes as if it's not a good thing. I'd love to have more money than I could spend," Billy said.

"I think Mr. Sage will spend every penny of it and more," Susan replied grimly.

"Really? That's a lot of money! I've never met anyone who had so much afore."

"Yes. It is a lot." She turned the subject back to her predicament. "I thought I would be undone when he lifted my arm," Susan said with a shudder. She'd been awake, thankfully, for she might have shouted out in surprise if he'd handled her so roughly when she was asleep.

"I didn't want to leave the cabin but couldn't argue against their instructions. The captain would cuss me, and I'd probably get a flogging for disobeying orders. The captain says the nobs are paying him well, so he wants to keep them happy. He wouldn't be pleased if they were angry with me."

Susan winced at his words. "Billy, promise me that you won't put yourself in danger on my account. I don't wish you to be in trouble because of me."

"But they're going to force you to marry, and you can't want that, surely?"

"No. I don't," Susan said. For all hope would be lost, she inwardly acknowledged. There was only one man she had ever loved, and that was Miles. That he'd never looked at her as anything other than his sister's friend didn't alter her feelings. If she were forced into a marriage with Charles Sage her inner hopes would be dashed forever. She might know that in reality Miles would never marry her, but it didn't prevent her from dreaming.

Focusing back on Billy, she tried to make him understand. "They are stronger than us, and we have no other friends on board this ship. I will try to stop the wedding when I'm onshore, but I'm not hopeful that I will be able to. I imagine they will employ a clergyman who has little issue with marrying a reluctant bride. I'm not foolish enough to risk my life, or yours, to try to escape. We can't do so from our situation here, so I will accept my fate at the moment."

"You're very brave," Billy said.

"I'm not. I'm just trying to be practical." Susan blinked away a tear. She felt anything but confident in her ability to remain calm and pragmatic. "I will try to rescue you from this ship, though, when I do leave. I don't think you like life on board, do you?"

Billy flushed. "No. I thought being at sea would be a good life. But I seem to do everything wrong, so I'm always being beaten. Captain sometimes threatens to throw me overboard because he gets so angry with me, and I do try to be good, honest I do, 'cause I can't swim."

"Oh! You poor thing!" Susan responded. If the worst came to the worst, the least she would do was somehow release her young saviour from his drudgery.

Chapter 4

Miles reached the barracks some time after the two hours had passed, with Dunn by his side. Jones was already waiting for them.

"Well?" Miles asked his friend.

"Seems he's in dun territory good and proper. Owes some blunt to almost everyone he's come into contact with, then he avoids them like the plague! He's a sly one; wouldn't trust him as far as I could throw him," Jones responded.

"Very motivated for his scheme to come to fruition then," Miles said, his tone dark. "We've had some luck. He's definitely with Sage. They've taken a ship – the *Dolphin* – to Scotland. It's no surprise, as that's what they intended doing with my sister. Speaking to a young lad who works on the ship next to where they were docked proved fruitful. Seems they're aiming to sail to Burnmouth, which is just over the border but on the east coast, nowhere near Gretna."

"The deuced maggot!" Jones exclaimed. "Have you hired a boat?"

"No. They've a day's sailing ahead of me," Miles said. "I'm going to ride across country. Hopefully I'll catch up with them before it's too late."

"That'll be a hard ride," Jones pointed out. "And a damned fight when you get there. They aren't going to hand her over willingly."

"I'll be armed and prepared," Miles said.

Jones looked at Dunn and smiled. "Looks like we're going on an adventure. We shall be modern-day knights of the round table."

Dunn laughed. "Always did fancy yourself as a knight in shining armour, Jones. Just concentrate on bringing everything you might need. We'll be travelling without your valet."

"There's always a downside to being gallant," Jones replied. "So inconvenient, but a young lady needs rescuing, and there aren't three better fellows the length of the country who will do it with the style and finesse we shall."

"Thank you," Miles said. "I'll be grateful to have your company on the journey and your eyes on my back when the fight starts."

"It will be as it always has been, my friend," Dunn said.

"It has," Miles responded, a lifetime of meaning and memories behind the words.

"I refuse to bivouac though," Jones said. "Those days are definitely behind me."

"How did you cope in the Peninsula?" Miles asked, amused.

"With great fortitude, my friend, which the great Wellington could instil in a fellow, even when he was young Wellesley," Jones said seriously. "Now, though, I have standards I refuse to compromise on. We'll be ready to go in an hour."

"I shall return then," Miles said, readying himself to leave the barracks. "Thank you, my friends."

*

35

A rushed note to his mother was all that Miles had the time to leave. There would be recriminations, but he couldn't delay his departure to pacify a clinging parent. She had behaved abominably towards his sister when Edith had refused to marry the men her mother had chosen for her, so there was little chance that Lady Longdon would sympathise with Susan's plight if he were foolish enough to mention the truth behind his sudden journey.

Wrapped in his greatcoat, bags packed and secured to his horse, he set off back to the barracks. A plan of action in his mind and determined to rescue Susan at all costs, he had not felt so focused in a long time.

His two friends were waiting, already mounted on their own fine horses. Wrapped in thick woollen greatcoats, each was prepared for the hard ride that lay ahead. Hundreds of miles would need to be covered in the fastest way possible if they were to help Susan.

"Ready?" Miles asked as soon as he arrived.

"Always," came the double reply, and the horses were spurred into action. Their journey had begun.

*

The route to the first overnight stop was always going to be the shortest part of the journey. They'd started out extremely late, and it wasn't ideal to travel at night at the speeds they needed to maintain. They were in little danger of being accosted by footpads, as the three of them were grouped together and heavily armed, but although they took the main roads, there was always the chance of stumbling over a hole in the road.

At Harlow, Miles called a halt to their travels. They knocked the innkeeper up, but he was amenable to having three of his rooms filled by men who were willing to pay in advance. After arranging a very early breakfast, they separated and fell onto their beds, not bothering to change into nightclothes.

Dawn had barely broken when Miles left his chamber, still yawning. He grimaced at Dunn, who was at the top of the stairs. "I'm not used to getting up with the lark anymore. I'll be asleep on my horse later."

"You never could take the pace. Old before your time," Dunn said, tripping down the stairs as refreshed as always.

Miles followed him, muttering darkly, which increased as he walked into the tap room to see Jones already tucking into a bowl of hot porridge, with pieces of thick, warm bread at his side.

"Thought I was going to have to wake you two up," Jones said, scraping out his empty bowl. "Food here is delicious. Fill up."

"I thought I had a healthy appetite, but you really are a stomach on legs," Miles said with a shake of his head, pouring himself a cup of coffee. "You should be the size of the Regent the way you eat."

"He doesn't have my hobbies," Jones replied enigmatically.

"It's too early to start talking about your depraved habits," Dunn said with a groan.

"There's nothing depraved about being a popular escort about town."

"With married women," Miles interjected.

"They are the safest kind," Jones said with a smile.

"Until you upset a husband one day. How many brats have been born with golden locks when their fathers are dark haired?"

"Tsk, tsk. I would never risk a child of mine being brought up by any of the fops we are surrounded by. Give me some credit, my friend."

Shaking his head, Miles tucked into the food laid out for them. He'd missed the camaraderie being with his fellow officers brought. Being enlisted into the cavalry was all he'd ever wanted; it was purely circumstance that had put paid to his dream. He was glad the wars were over, but nothing had ever given him the sense of doing something worthwhile more than fighting for his country. To be back with his fellow men was bittersweet.

The three set out on what was going to be a long day. He would not normally ride above ten to fifteen miles an hour, but the cavalry were trained to ride faster, around thirty miles an hour, or even faster when needed. Miles didn't think that sort of pace would be necessary, but he was determined to cover as much ground as possible by maintaining a faster pace than normal. Every moment counted on this journey.

*

Decamping to a hostelry on the outskirts of Doncaster was the end of a very long day for the riders. Each was quiet as they entered their rooms. The weather had been dry, but the dirt from the road couldn't be avoided. They had each worn a face scarf to try to reduce the amount of dirt settling on their skin, but when they first stepped into the inn, they didn't seem like the fine gentlemen they were.

A lot of warm water was used to try to wash some of the grime away before the three convened in the tap room of the inn. None of them were bothered about hiring a private parlour; life was far more interesting in a busy tap room, and they weren't going to be sitting around for hours wasting time.

"I don't think my greatcoat will ever come clean," Dunn repined. "It brings back nightmare memories of the red dust of the Peninsula."

"I'll buy you a new one." Miles grinned. "You always were too fastidious about your attire."

"One should always look well, even when going into battle," Dunn responded airily. "It was a damned inconvenience trying to restore one's uniform to its pristine state after any skirmish."

"You mean it was hard for your batman," Jones pointed out.

"I pay him well," Dunn said. "It would damage his reputation and his pride for me to be turned out shoddily."

"You'd think he was talking about attending a ball, instead of preparing for a battle," Jones said to Miles.

"I suppose it took his mind off what we had to face," Miles answered.

The men nodded in silence. They had all seen images no decent human being should be forced to witness. It was a miracle they'd all returned. Many of their friends hadn't.

"So, this wench," Jones started, changing the subject. "She's an heiress?"

"Yes. A decent family, although the stepmother is a harridan," Miles said. "Seems to hate her stepdaughter for no reason apart from her sheer existence. Edith had mentioned in the past how cruel they were to her friend, but I admit I didn't take it seriously. I soon realised my mistake when I called in to glean what information I could and found she'd been taken. Mrs. King was brutal even

39

though she knew her stepdaughter had been hurt in some way."

"Happens a lot. Probably jealous of a younger woman," Dunn said.

"Actually, I don't think it's that," Miles said. "If you compared them both purely on looks, the stepmother is by far the prettier, or would have been in her prime. Miss King is quite plain, but a pleasant girl."

"When one is reliant on the insipid word 'pleasant', it is clear the type of girl to which one refers!" Jones laughed. "Why are we saving this gargoyle? This will probably be her best chance at a match."

"Too harsh, Jones," Miles said quickly, flaring up in Susan's defence. "Not everyone can be a diamond, or stunningly beautiful, but that doesn't mean they should be forced into marriage with a scoundrel, or worse. Once he's married to her and accessed her fortune, goodness knows what fate will await the girl. I wouldn't wish that on anyone, let alone a gentlewoman."

Jones held up his hands. "I apologise. No need to eat me. She's clearly worth saving or I wouldn't be here."

"What happens if we get there too late?" Dunn asked.

Miles shrugged. "She becomes a widow very quickly."

"Is she worth being strung up for? Or at the very least transported," Dunn asked.

"I have a score to settle with the scoundrels who've taken her. They should have disappeared when they were foiled in trying to abduct Edith," Miles answered, his grey eyes darkening. "Trying their luck with a second innocent is a step neither will be walking away from."

"I think you need to calm down before we get there," Jones soothed. "Your Miss King doesn't deserve the guilt of destroying your family as well as her own because of all this."

"He's right," Dunn said. "There are going to be repercussions for her. Let's not add to her troubles."

"I'll try to contain myself," Miles promised.

Jones smiled. "Lunatic Longdon has made a promise to be sensible."

"I'm always sensible," Miles said.

"I remember you riding manically, hellbent on breaking the French line, on more than one occasion," Dunn said wryly.

"If in doubt, shock them," Miles responded with a grin. "A surprise charge stunned most of them into not even loading their weapons."

"That's not how I remember it," Dunn countered. "Mayhem and carnage, more like."

"Do you remember Wellington's face after Waterloo? He'd aged during that skirmish more than the others combined," Jones said.

"I think we all did," Miles said grimly. The scenes they'd witnessed still haunted him far more than he admitted. No one wanted to hear about the horrors of war and he couldn't blame them.

"It's hard returning home. I still hear the noise," Jones said, unusually sober.

"I've barely had a decent night's sleep since I came back," Miles admitted for the first time.

"The curse of going to war, I suppose," Dunn said. "Come! Enough of this melancholy! We have a girl to rescue and a tankard of ale to drink before we turn in."

Miles took a large swig of his beer. Talking about the battles would mean an even more troubled night's sleep. It was always the same. Faces, sounds and feelings, ensuring he woke up screaming in the night. Drink would have to deepen his sleep, for he could not wake his friends, even though they slept in different rooms. He knew how far he could normally be heard, from when worried staff had run to his aid in the early days of his return. No. Tonight he would not reveal what terrors lay for him in the dark. Indicating for his tankard to be refilled, he turned to his friends with a smile on his face. Regularity. That's what mattered. Pretending, just as they did, that life was orderly and people didn't do inflict upon each other the horrific deeds that he'd witnessed.

*

The next day they arose a little worse for wear, but it didn't stop them climbing onto their horses with the same gusto they'd had since they started. Good-natured teasing was thrown between them until they'd left the inn behind and gathered speed, removing any opportunity to speak. Horse changes were made with speed and the urgency to continue the momentum as far as possible. Only the finest horses would do. They might not be cavalry horses, but for the right price good quality horse-flesh could be obtained.

They barely rested until very late in the evening when they arrived at Alnwick. Groaning as they stepped into the inn, they secured rooms and lots of fresh warm water.

Once they'd washed most of the day's dirt off, they gathered downstairs as they had the previous night. Their clothes were looking travel weary, but there was little point in soiling clean clothing when time in the saddle was still required. Each was usually fastidious, but looking at them now, no one would imagine they weren't perfectly at ease in their dishevelled attire as they lounged in chairs pulled up to a large wooden table.

"My valet is going to cry over the state of my boots," Jones said, examining his footwear with a heartfelt sigh.

"A good thing he isn't with you." Dunn rolled his eyes in Miles's direction.

"I shall be forced to pay him a bonus this quarter," Jones mused. "I like these boots. I do hope they can be brought back to life."

"There are more important things to worry about," Miles said, but his tone held no reproof. They all had ways of coping with situations that they didn't like; Jones's fastidiousness and quips were his.

"Than my boots, dear fellow? There is nothing more important than maintaining one's standards. We aren't in the wilds of Spain now. We could be *seen*!"

"What's the plan for tomorrow? We're going to cross the border sometime during the morning if we set off as early as we have been doing," Dunn said.

"Yes. Another early start and straight to the harbour at Burnmouth. Apparently, it's only a small fishing village, so it should be easy to track them down," Miles replied. He tried not to think of what Susan had endured whilst they were travelling towards her.

"If they're off the ship, it will make our lives easier," Jones said.

"Since when haven't you liked a challenge?" Miles asked in mock disgust.

"Since I've decided I'd like to grow old, rather than die a spectacular but terribly wasteful death."

"He's gone boring in his old age," Dunn said, crossing his legs at the ankles. He would usually admire his boots in his unaffected way when seated in that position, but looking at them in their current state would lead him to repine their state.

"So I see," Miles said.

"I'm actually the youngest of the three of us," Jones pointed out.

"You don't look it," came Dunn's quick response.

"Offensive brat."

Chapter 5

Susan awoke to find the cabin bathed in moonlight and the ship still. No noise could be heard; the dull sounds of a crew of men working day and night unusually absent. She tried to move, but a wave of dizziness made her lay her head on her pillow and take deep breaths to calm the nausea.

When she had steadied herself, she realised that, unfortunately, she had only one option. "Billy?" she whispered into the darkness.

Billy's crumpled form was snuggled under his blanket and at first didn't respond to Susan's whispers. Only when Susan raised her voice slightly did he start to stir.

"Billy. I need your help," Susan said urgently.

"Uh? What?" Billy mumbled, finally sitting up in bed. Rubbing his eyes and gathering his wits, he moved to Susan. "What is it, miss?"

"I need to— I, er, need to use the pot," Susan said, glad the dark shielded her blushing cheeks.

"Oh."

"Yes. Oh," Susan responded with a wry smile. "I've tried to move, but I feel so dizzy when I do so. I'm afraid I'll need your help to climb off the bed."

"I'll bring the pot to you," Billy said, ever practical.

Susan was mortified. "Then you'll have to move it."

"It's only what I do with the captain," Billy said. "When he's been onshore, he can never walk to the pot."

"I see," Susan said. "Can I try to walk first?"

"I'd rather you didn't," Billy said. "If you faint, it will cause a heck of a noise. Mr. Sage and Mr. Malone sleep in the next cabin to us."

"In that case, please bring me the pot," Susan said. "I don't want them to know I'm awake."

Billy silently brought the much-needed item, and although he helped Susan off the bed, he turned away while she made herself comfortable.

Almost falling onto the bed with dizziness once the deed had been done, Susan let out a groan. "I've been lying down for too long. My legs feel they won't uphold me."

Billy didn't speak until he'd put everything back in order. "You might hear some new noises later," he said.

"Why? What's going on?" Susan asked, alert to the reluctant note in Billy's voice.

"We've docked," Billy answered.

Susan drew a sharp intake of breath. "In Scotland?"

"Yes."

"Then it will soon be over," Susan said, deflated.

Billy tried to be positive. "They don't know you're awake yet."

"I won't fool them forever. They're already getting suspicious."

"I'll do all that I can to delay them," Billy said bravely.

Susan reached for his hands. They were cold, rough to the touch and small. He might be fifteen, but he could easily be mistaken for a younger child. "You have done more than enough. There aren't enough thank-yous in the world to express my gratitude, but I don't want you putting yourself at risk on my account. I can accept my fate far more easily knowing that you haven't been hurt as a result of my not wishing to be married to whichever of them is to be my husband."

"They're not nice men, miss. You wouldn't have a happy time of it," Billy said.

"I know. But we'd need an army of men to get off this ship in one piece. We can't do anything to stop them. I need you to understand that, Billy. Promise me you won't do anything rash," Susan demanded, her voice quiet, but insistent.

"I won't," Billy promised, but Susan would worry about him until the nightmare was over.

*

Mid-morning brought Charles and Albert into the cabin. Both were impatient now they'd arrived at their destination. Charles pushed Billy aside and strode over to where Susan lay. She was sleeping, but Charles noticed a difference in her.

"She has no fever. Why didn't you tell me?" he demanded of Billy.

"It might come back," Billy said meekly. "I've seen it happen afore."

"That doesn't matter, you damned fool! As long as we're married, I'll get her fortune." Charles seemed intent on inflicting a blow on Billy, but something on the table caught his eye. He reached for the jug of water and threw it over Susan.

Exclaiming in surprise, Susan woke up, shocked and spluttering. As she wiped the water from her eyes, she saw the grim expressions of her two captors.

"Good morning," Charles said with false pleasantry. "I thought you'd wish to be awake as soon as possible on your wedding day."

Susan didn't respond. She wouldn't give them the satisfaction of knowing she was terrified. She just watched them warily.

"Ah, she's all coy," Charles said, turning to Albert. "Come, help me escort her to Carson. He'll marry us as soon as we arrive."

Susan scuttled over the bed to the wall of the cabin, trying to put some distance between herself and her captors. "No! Please!" she said, grasping a blanket for protection.

"Don't be afraid, my dear. I'm going to look after you for the rest of your life from today," Charles said with a cold grin. "For however long that life is."

"Leave her be!" Billy stepped in front of the bed, but, with one fist, Charles sent him reeling.

"Get out of my way, you vermin, and stay out of it."

Susan choked on a sob as Billy's body lay prone on the floor. He'd promised to keep himself safe, and yet he'd still tried to save her. "You shouldn't have done that," she said. "He's naught but a child."

"He'll know in future to keep his nosey beak out of other people's business," Charles said without remorse. "Now, come. Enough trying to obstruct what's inevitable. It won't work. You're to be married, and that's the end of it."

It wouldn't do to try to hinder their plans. For what would she be delaying for? Nothing or no one was coming to her rescue; Susan knew it without doubt. While she was on the ship there was no escape. She wasn't convinced there would be whilst travelling to whatever church they planned on taking her, but she would try to do something to foil their plans. Otherwise all hope was lost, and that was too upsetting a thought for her to face in her weakened state.

She didn't struggle when Charles grabbed her arm and roughly pulled her to the edge of the bed. With her injured arm, Susan tried to steady herself.

"I feel a little light-headed," she said as Charles roughly swung her legs over the edge.

"Albert, for God's sake, help me! She's a dead weight."

"How rude you are, Mr. Sage. You are no gentleman," Susan said, before crumpling into Charles's arms in a dead faint.

"Good God! Is there nothing easy in this life?" Charles cursed as he pushed Susan back onto the bed, her head thudding against the cabin wall from the force of his movement.

"We'll never get her to the clergyman," Albert said. "Perhaps the boy is right and she's still ill."

"I don't give a damn. This journey has taken enough of our time. I want the deed done, and then I can start planning my future," Charles said.

"Our future," Albert said.

"That goes without saying," Charles responded quickly, his tone sharp. "You need to bring Carson here. He'll perform the ceremony on board," he said of the most unprincipled clergyman he'd been able to find when he'd planned to marry Edith.

"He might refuse to perform the service if she's barely conscious," Albert warned.

"She can sit on a chair," Charles replied. "One way or another, I'm getting married today."

"I'll be as quick as I can," Albert said, turning on his heel.

Albert returned within the hour. Following him was a clergyman who, although looking uncomfortable, was willing to carry out the service for the right price. As it had been agreed in advance for the proposed kidnapping of Miles's sister, he'd been long expecting the arrival of Charles and a reluctant bride.

Charles stood as they entered the room. Susan was still lying down; she was conscious, but her pallor was ghostly white. She turned her head as the door opened, and tears sprang to her eyes. It was over. An image of Miles entered her head: he was laughing at something, his grey eyes sparkling as they did very often. Blinking the tears and the image away, she sighed. There was no point in longing for what couldn't have been even if her kidnap hadn't happened. He had never been hers. It was the foolish hope of a girl who should have known better. People like her didn't have happy endings. She'd realised that many years ago, once her stepmother's taunting had started.

"Mr. Carson, glad you could join us. My future wife has been ill. Seasickness, you know, but we are keen to marry," Charles said smoothly.

Susan looked at the clergyman pleadingly.

"Her arm is injured and her dress is torn," the clergyman said. A reluctant bride was one thing; this seemed to be an even more suspicious situation.

"An unfortunate accident, which I'm sure your increased fee will ensure you overlook," Charles replied.

"Stop being keen to spend our money," Albert muttered.

Charles shot a glare at his friend but chose not to respond.

"You'll need two witnesses," Mr. Carson said, looking in concern at the scene he was faced with. His expression was wary on spying Billy's prone body on the floor, but he didn't make any comment about it.

"Fetch one of the ship's crew, or wake the boy," Charles instructed Albert.

"You could always stir yourself," Albert grumbled. "I'd like to remind you that I'm an equal partner in all of this."

"Not quite," Charles said.

Albert squared up to his friend. "Now wait a minute. We're in this together. I got the chit; I arranged where we were to sail to. I found the clergyman. You arranged the ship. As it stands, I'm doing most of the work and you are trying to lord it over me. I won't have it."

"Oh, will you not?" Charles said, a dangerous glint in his eye.

"No. It was an equal partnership we entered into," Albert said. "We agreed that from the start."

Charles turned to the clergyman. "Are you squeamish?"

"Me? No?" came the puzzled response.

"Good. Albert, you've been annoying the life out of me for a long time. Goodbye," Charles said, and with one fluid movement, he brought a gun from his rear waistband and shot Albert in the chest.

Hardly able to register a look of surprise, Albert's dead body slumped to the ground.

Susan screamed and Billy scurried into the corner, his pretence of being still unconscious gone. Rolling himself

51

into a tight ball, he hid his face, hoping he wouldn't be the next victim.

Mr. Carson swallowed and stepped back towards the door.

Charles looked at him and smiled mockingly. "You don't need to worry. I have some morals, which include inflicting no harm on a man of the cloth."

"Was there really any need to kill him?" Mr. Carson asked, a little braver after Charles's words.

"When you've put up with him for as long as I have, yes, there was. Now, shall we get this wedding done? I don't want to waste any more time. There have been enough delays."

"There still need to be two witnesses," Mr. Carson said.

"You, boy," Charles instructed Billy. "Go and get two shipmates, and don't be slow about it, or you'll end the same way as he has," he said, indicating Albert with his gun.

Billy scrambled to his feet, and with an apologetic glance towards Susan, he left the room.

Charles nonchalantly reloaded his gun; he smiled at Susan as she watched his actions. "Always best to be prepared, my dear. Saves a lot of arguing when one's opponents know one mean business."

"Shouldn't we move his body out of the room at least?" Mr. Carson asked, nodding at Albert's corpse.

"No. You can combine the two. A wedding and a funeral, although if he gets into heaven there's hope for us all," Charles responded with a chuckle. He glanced at Susan. "I had no intention of him living with us, but he never doubted my word. Why share your fortune when I have no need to? The fool believed everything I said. A wonder he survived the battles he fought in, he was such an idiot.

Although I don't suppose you need brains on the battlefield, just the ability to blindly do what the officers tell you. I'd never have put myself at risk without argument."

"You have no remorse, have you?" Susan asked, finally finding her voice and her anger.

"No. He was in the way and had to go. A prudent lesson to keep in mind, my dear. We shall rub along perfectly if you are one who learns quickly. I have no patience with those who don't."

"You're despicable," Susan spat.

"Probably, but I'm soon to be your husband, so I'd start minding that sharp tongue of yours," Charles said pleasantly. "Or there will be repercussions, which you won't like. I promise you."

"How can you allow this?" Susan turned her stare onto the clergyman. "You know I'm not a willing participant. It's clear I've been brought here against my will, and yet you are going to marry us, aren't you?"

Mr. Carson looked away from Susan but didn't answer her.

"One day you'll have to account for this," Susan said. "There will be a time when you'll have to answer for your deeds."

"Oh, shut up!" Charles cursed. "Or I'll be a widower sooner rather than later."

"Am I going to get out of this cabin alive?" Susan asked, sure that dying before the marriage was consummated would be a good thing.

"Oh yes. We have a trip to London to enjoy first of all, to ensure your finances are in order. We'll soon have the paperwork stating that, as your legal husband, I become responsible for your fortune," Charles said. "After that, who knows? Many women die in childbirth, or have accidents out riding, or suffer something so simple as falling down the stairs."

Susan shuddered. She wasn't surprised, but it was worse than she'd thought. As soon as he was able to access her funds, she was expendable. She was no fool. A man like Sage wouldn't think twice about arranging an accident for her. Having not thought it possible, she realised her future had just become even bleaker, for she would have to endure her husband forcing himself on her. He would ensure the marriage was legal before they reached London. She had no idea how she could face that.

"Where is that damned boy?" Charles growled.

"I'm here, sir!" Billy said, entering the cabin and immediately flattening himself against the wall.

"Well, where are the two witnesses?" Charles demanded, waving his gun in Billy's direction.

"Three are coming," Billy said.

"Three? I only need two," Charles said.

"But it would be such a shame to separate my friends and me. They so want to give you what you deserve," said the pleasant voice of Miles as he filled the door, his gun pointing directly at Charles.

Chapter 6

The air stilled, but as soon as Charles saw Miles, he reacted by pointing his gun at Susan and just as quickly pulling a second gun out of his waistband, which he pointed at Miles.

"Don't be a fool, or she dies," he said.

Miles moved into the cabin to allow Jones and Dunn to follow him. They all took in the scene whilst pointing their weapons at Charles.

"I think you'd better leave," Miles said to the clergyman, who looked fit to collapse. "There will be no wedding today."

"Stay where you are!" Charles said. "Or you'll end up like him." He nodded towards Albert. The clergyman remained fixed in position, too terrified to move.

"Rather cosy in here, isn't it?" Jones said as pleasantly as if he were attending a ball or rout.

"How the devil did you get past the ship's company?" Charles demanded.

"It's surprising how a fistful of notes will focus the minds of a handful of sailors. They promised not to return until nightfall. That's plenty of time for us to finish our business here and leave." Miles looked bedraggled and travel weary, but his tone was calm and self-assured.

"Damn turncoats," Charles spat.

"Miss King, would you like to slowly move towards me?" Miles asked calmly, as if he were merely asking for a dance, or passing the time of day.

"She goes nowhere," Charles said through a clenched jaw. "You might have weapons aimed at me, but I'm competent enough to fire before I'm done for, and this gun is prone to going off with the slightest pressure. I can already feel my finger getting tired. I would suggest you lower your own weapons if you want your friend here not to have another hole in her. One of the more fatal kind this time. I will guarantee it."

Miles cursed under his breath, but he could see Charles's finger twitching. There was a good chance the blaggard was speaking the truth, and although Charles would most certainly die in the gunfight, Susan was at risk. Sighing, he nodded to his friends. "Lower your weapons."

"Glad to see you're a sensible man."

When the weapons were lowered Charles slowly moved across the cabin. Everyone watched him like a hawk. Standing at Susan's side, he indicated that she should move off the bed.

"She'll faint again!" Billy cried out. "She's still ill."

"Billy, shush," Susan said, speaking for the first time. "It's fine. Stay where you are."

Susan's legs did wobble, and she stumbled into a faint the moment she was upright, but Charles threw his second gun on the bed, hooked his arm under Susan's and dragged her to him. He pointed the gun to her temple.

"This is better," he said. "I never did like uneven odds. Not unless they are in my favour, of course."

Miles gritted his teeth. This was not part of the plan. Susan was more at risk now than she'd been before they'd arrived. At least then she was only going to be wed; now she was the hostage of a man who would have no compunction about killing her. For Charles would know his chances of leaving the cabin unhurt and free would be slim. He had nothing left to lose.

"You'll never get away," Miles said, unable to sound calm when his mind was racing over how best to protect Susan.

"Oh, I think you're wrong there. Boy, open that window wide," Charles said to Billy.

Billy looked at Miles for instruction, and on receiving a slight nod, he moved to the decorative window on the stern of the ship.

"It's a long way down," Dunn said warningly.

"And the tide is low," Jones added.

"I have little choice, as I'll never be allowed to walk out of this room alive," Charles responded.

"No, you won't," Miles said.

"Exactly. So, this obliging young lady is going to be my shield." Charles dragged Susan to the window. It was clear she was barely conscious; her limbs were limp and her head flopped to the side.

Charles struggled, but the three remained still. Although their guns were in easy reach, they were not about to risk Susan jerking as she tried to regain consciousness and being shot by one of their weapons. Reaching the window, Charles slung one leg over it and, with a fluid movement, pushed Susan into the room, fired his gun and fell below.

Jones and Dunn dove towards the door and ran out, aiming to reach Charles before he made his escape on shore. Miles had rushed forward, attempting to catch Susan before she crumpled to the floor. Billy and Mr. Carson had thrown themselves on the wooden floor to avoid the gunfire.

Lifting Susan into his arms, Miles tried to check her over. The wound on her arm was bleeding at the rough treatment it had suffered, and her head still lolled to the side in a faint.

He placed her gently on the bed and tried to make her comfortable. "Billy, that's your name, isn't it? Fetch some water and fresh bandages," Miles said. "And do you know of any laudanum on board?"

"Yes, sir, there is some. I'll do anything you wish if it'll help Miss," Billy said, moving to the door.

"Good. Fetch it to me. She's had a shock and will need to remain quiet, and her wound needs to be kept still."

Covering Susan with a rough blanket, Miles gently brushed her bedraggled curls out of the way. She looked sickly, but also young. His insides tugged at the thought she could so easily have been hurt. She had always looked so self-contained and elegant when he'd seen her – a serious woman, he'd always thought. Now, in the bed, she looked a vulnerable young girl, and he ached at what she must have gone through.

Billy returned to the room and, stepping over Albert's corpse with hardly a glance at the dead man, he handed Miles a small jar of laudanum and placed a jug of water on the table next to the bed. "I can tend her dressing," he said. "I've been looking after her."

"Thank you, Billy," Miles said. "I'll do it for now, but I can see you know your stuff when binding a wound."

Billy swelled a little under the praise. "The captain said I was to look after anyone who was ill, for I was no good for nowt else," he admitted. "I learned that the binding needs to be tight but not too tight for the bleeding to stop."

"Yes. I'll need a fresh bandage."

"I had to use her petticoat," Billy said with a flush. "She didn't mind when she woke."

Miles smiled. "That's a good thing, as I'm going to be forced to do the same."

Apologising to the semi-conscious Susan, he cut another length off her now shorter petticoat. Trying to use her outer dress as a cover for her legs, he concentrated on the fabric as he cut. He soothed her moans as he bathed and redressed her wound, then he lifted her head and indicated that Billy should pass him the phial of laudanum.

"Miss King, Susan," he said gently. "You need to swallow this. It will help you rest and keep you still. Your arm has suffered today."

"She's had a bad fever," Billy told him.

"Then this is doubly important because we don't want another one," Miles said, his attention still on Susan.

Her eyes fluttered open, and she gazed into the grey eyes which looked into hers. She would know those eyes anywhere, for she had dreamed of them for years. "You came," she said quietly.

"I did," Miles said with a small smile. "Now drink this."

Susan did as she was bid, grimacing at the taste of the liquid.

"It will help," Miles soothed. "When you've rested, we can make plans to return you home."

"I'm ruined," she said, blinking back tears.

"We can keep it quiet," Miles assured her. "It hasn't been too many days that you've been away."

"My stepmother," Susan said. She seemed determined to speak, but it was costing her. "She has never been able to keep a secret if it doesn't benefit her. She will relish this."

59

Miles couldn't argue against her observations after the little he'd seen of Mrs. King. "My mother is exactly the same, but your stepmother won't add to your ruination. It wouldn't benefit her."

"If it meant I was cut off from my father, she would," Susan said sadly. "Thank you for coming. Being ostracised is better than what I was facing. I never lost hope that you'd save me. Not until a few moments before you arrived."

"I'm glad you clung onto hope." Miles had too often seen what it meant when hope was lost. It was as effective as putting a gun to one's head on a battlefield. Where there was no hope, there was little chance of survival. "And I'm very relieved I didn't let you down."

"Never. I knew you of all people would help me if you could. You are the best of men," Susan said with a small smile. Miles swallowed an unexpected lump in his throat.

He laid her down as she drifted off, then stood and looked around the room. "We need to move Malone," he said in Mr. Carson's direction.

"I'm afraid I won't be able to help. Mr. Sage aimed well with his shot," Mr. Carson's feeble voice responded.

Miles turned more fully towards the clergyman, who was slumped in a chair. "Bloody hell!" he cursed as he walked to the injured man. "Where are you shot?"

"Here." Mr. Carson removed his bloodied hand from his thigh.

"You'll probably survive, but we'll have to get you off this ship."

"I'll probably survive?" came Mr. Carson's anguished cry.

"It'll perhaps teach you to be more circumspect about whose commissions you undertake. I hope they paid you well," Miles said without any compassion.

"I was to be paid at the end of the service."

"You have been served well then."

"I need a doctor," Mr. Carson begged.

"How did you travel here?"

"By carriage. It should still be on the dock."

"Aye, there was one when we came aboard," Miles recollected. "Billy, go and find Mr. Carson's groom and tell him to come and help his master. He needs a doctor when he gets home."

"I could bleed to death on the journey!"

"That is not my concern." Miles shrugged. "The sooner you're away from me the better. I despise you for what you were willing to be a part of today. Your bishop will be told of your conduct. I doubt he'll look favourably on it."

Mr. Carson looked set to speak but was interrupted by the return of Jones and Dunn.

"You don't bring good news," Miles said, looking at the set of their faces.

"No. The varlet has escaped. How the blazes he managed it, I have no idea," Jones said.

"I can only think he didn't surface after jumping in," Dunn offered.

"The mud can be deep in these parts," Mr. Carson offered, trying in a feeble way to gain some favour.

Jones shuddered dramatically. "What a way to die."

"The more horrible the better for him," Miles said.

"My dear Longdon, you have gone barbaric since you left the fold of the cavalry. I don't know what has come over you," Jones responded. "Now, what do we do with Malone's body?"

"Take him to the jetty and send for the magistrate," Miles said.

They were interrupted by Mr. Carson's coachman, who entered the room with Billy, looking very wary. He stumbled at the sight of Albert's body.

"Come in, you're in no danger," Miles assured him. "I just want you to get your master home. He needs a doctor."

"Yes, sir," the coachman quietly replied. Pulling Mr. Carson's arm around his own shoulder, he led his wounded employer out. Mr. Carson shot Miles a look of disgust but said nothing as he left the cabin.

"I'm afraid he won't be putting in a good word for you with the Almighty from that expression," Dunn said with a laugh in his voice.

"I won't cry myself to sleep over it," Miles said dryly. "Now, give me a hand with Albert. I know Jones doesn't like to get his hands dirty."

"It wastes the time I spend looking after them," Jones said, gazing at his fingers with approval. "I was made for the finer things in life."

"Is this the same man who rode across Spain and the Americas with us?" Dunn lifted Albert's feet at the same time as Miles hooked his arms under Albert's.

"He's gone soft since Waterloo," Miles said with amusement. "And Albert must have put on weight since then! I'm tempted to just throw him overboard."

The two men struggled with their heavy load but eventually deposited him on the dock. Billy hovered around them.

"You need to find the harbour master, Billy, and tell him what's happened," Miles said.

"Yes, sir," Billy said, eager to do Miles's bidding. But, faltering, he turned back, a little worried. "When the captain returns, sir—"

"He won't lay a finger on you while I'm here," Miles promised, knowing instinctively what the boy was worried about.

Billy smiled and ran off in the direction of the buildings in which harbour business was carried out.

Frowning, Miles returned to the cabin.

"What's troubling you, my friend?" Jones asked amiably.

"We have a damsel who is in no fit state to travel, and yet she needs to be returned to her family as soon as possible."

"Yes. We didn't plan what was going to happen once we charged in and rescued our fair maiden," Jones said, glancing at Susan's sleeping form. "On a positive note, we made it in time."

"Yes, thankfully we did. I'd have preferred it not to have been as close as it was though," Miles admitted.

"I'd say it was perfect timing for a dramatic entrance."

Miles shook his head at his friend. "You worry me sometimes, you really do. I think the best plan would be to sail back with her," he said, musing through the options to himself.

"Days on a boat? With a rapscallion crew?" Jones asked incredulously.

"Afraid you'll be thrown overboard when we're out at sea?" Miles countered with a laugh. "They've shown they have loyalty to the highest bidders – look how soon they deserted Sage. You'll be perfectly safe."

"Surely there are other alternatives?"

"Of course there are, but do you wish to volunteer to make up the story to explain why a young lady who is injured and recovering from a fever is travelling alone with three men? For we'll need one every night we stop, and it will take us longer to travel by road in a carriage," Miles pointed out. "The sooner we get Miss King home the better."

"Always the voice of reason," Dunn said with a smile.

"That's why I came out of our adventures unscathed. Plan realistically first, then act," Miles said smugly.

Dunn sighed. "I can't believe those words came from Lunatic Longdon. I think he has a superiority problem now he's lord of the manor."

"Not I," Miles said. "Added to that, though, my own leg is complaining bitterly about the riding we've done over the last few days."

"What have you been doing to your leg?"

"Had an argument with a footpad from which, although I won, I didn't come off unscathed," Miles admitted, remembering the fight that he was lucky to have survived. A gunshot wound and a stab wound had both missed vital organs and bones. Not many would recover as quickly as he had from such an encounter.

"The circle you socialise in leaves a lot to be desired, Longdon," Jones scoffed.

"It's a story for another time. To get back to the issue we're faced with at the moment, it seems, unfortunately, sailing home is the best idea," Dunn said. "She's not fit to travel hundreds of miles in a carriage."

Miles glanced at the bed. "No. When Billy returns, we'll put him back in charge of her, and then we shall await the arrival of the crew." Seeing Susan so vulnerable made his insides ache.

"I think we'll be in for a long wait, with the amount of money you gave them," Jones said. "Then we'll have to remain moored up while they sober up."

"We could always try sailing the thing ourselves," Dunn suggested.

"That would involve Jones getting his hands dirty," Miles pointed out, he was glad the banter distracted him from his unexpected feelings towards Susan.

"We shall be waiting until the crew are fit to sail," Jones said firmly. "I have some standards that are unnegotiable."

Chapter 7

Susan awoke to the feel of the ship swaying with more momentum then it had been whilst in port. She blinked, and although she felt groggy and there was a dull ache in her shoulder, she didn't feel as detached from the world as she had after the fever had broken.

Looking around the cabin, she was surprised to see Miles sitting at the table reading a newspaper.

"Lord Longdon?" she asked, her voice a little croaky.

"Ah, so you're back with us, are you? Splendid." Miles folded the paper and placed it on the table. "We thought you were going to sleep the whole journey."

"How long have I slept?"

"What remained of yesterday, all last night, and we are just after three of the clock in the afternoon. Quite a time! I was beginning to think I'd overdosed you with laudanum," Miles said affably.

"You must think me extremely indolent," Susan said with a stretch. She winced when moving her injured arm.

"Not at all." Miles poured her a glass of water. "You do need to be careful with that wound, though. It's been knocked about because of your rough treatment and has reopened. I've patched it up as best I can, but if you can try not to move it, it would be for the best."

"Thank you. I'm sorry to have caused so much trouble," Susan said. "But there was no one else I could turn to when I first saw Mr. Malone loitering around my abode."

"I'm glad you did, or you'd be facing a very different future," Miles said, helping her to raise herself a little so she could have the drink.

When sated, Susan was relieved to rest her head on the pillows once more. She'd never been so close to Miles, and the feel of him supporting her in the crook of his shoulder caused her to blush vividly. "It would have been a very short future, from what Mr. Sage hinted at."

"Men like him get away with preying on innocents," Miles said, his jaw clenched. "Your family will be happy to see your return."

An expression of sadness flashed across Susan's features. Taking hold of the hand on her uninjured arm, he gave it a gentle squeeze. "Your father was worried about you and will be relieved when you return. I have a difficult mother, so I understand some of your troubles with your stepmother, but although I accept your fears, I'm sure in reality she doesn't want to see you ruined."

"Perhaps not. She never thought I'd marry but has set a time limit of the end of the month for my finding a husband. It was supposed to be the end of the season, but just before all this happened, she lost patience with me and reduced the amount of time she was willing for me to remain at home."

Miles recalled the words Mrs. King had uttered regarding a kidnapping being her stepdaughter's best chance at a marriage. "My sister was put under an inordinate amount of pressure from my own mother about marrying. I expect she told you about it."

"Edith and I were surprised at how similar our experiences were," Susan said. "I've missed her greatly since her marriage but can't repine, because she finally found the right man to love."

"Yes, I wasn't sure about the match at first, but Ralph is a good man and is besotted with Edith, which is all I'd want in a husband for her," Miles acknowledged. It had been difficult for him to accept Ralph, even though the man was his friend. He'd thought at first Ralph was toying with his sister, and only time had shown him that there was true feeling underneath Ralph's cool exterior.

"Could I make yet another imposition on you?" Susan asked.

"Of course."

"I'd rather send a note to my father to say I'm no longer in any danger and ask you to deliver me to my aunt. She lives in Chelsea and will know how best to plan for my future. This escapade has taught me that I need to do something positive about how I want to live my life," Susan said.

"Will your father accept you going to your aunt? I'd imagine he'd want you to be with him after what you've been through."

"He won't contradict Aunt Florence. She's his sister, and he's terrified of her."

"I know the feeling," Miles said dryly, his eyes dancing with amusement.

Susan laughed quietly. "It would be unjust for me to report your comment to Edith, because of the service you've done for me, but know that I'm very tempted."

Miles smiled. "I now know precisely why you and Edith get on so well." He noticed Susan's eyelids closing. "You are tired. Time to rest now. There's no point overexerting yourself on the homeward journey. We want you to arrive as well as you can after suffering from a fever. I wouldn't wish you to have any sort of relapse."

"I just feel a feeble woman," Susan said. "I've never had a day of illness in my life, and I'm struggling with feeling so weak and dependent on everyone."

"Just enjoy being looked after while you can. None of us is suffering from exertion on this voyage."

"Are the ship's crew trustworthy? Billy doesn't describe them at all favourably," Susan said, fighting to keep her eyes open.

Miles rested his hand on her shoulder. "There's absolutely nothing to worry about. Rest."

The feel of his hand, warm and firm but gentle, soothed her worries instantly. He would protect them. She had nothing to worry about whilst he was there. "Thank you."

It wasn't many minutes before Miles moved away from Susan, assured she was sleeping peacefully. Her anxiety was understandable, and he would do everything in his power to ensure she was safe.

Pondering over her family life, he shook his head. How could a young woman who seemed to have everything actually be, in truth, so very lonely? She was bereft of the affection of her family, apart from her father? Edith thought highly of Susan, and his sister was no fool in choosing those she regarded. A pity her own family couldn't value her worth.

Picking up his paper, he sat down once more. It wasn't of his concern. He would deliver her safely, and then his duty was done. If he felt annoyance that she might be forced into a suitable but unhappy marriage, it wasn't his affair. However, Susan's future continued to niggle at his insides while she slept peacefully.

*

On the second day of the return course, Susan insisted she wanted to go above deck. Billy helped her to climb from the bed and sit in a chair for a little while, watching as he carried warm water into the room so she could wash.

"I would like a bath, but I know that is too much to ask." Susan smiled at Billy's horrified expression. "Don't worry, I'm not expecting you to fill a bath full of water."

"It's not that, miss. Why would you want to have a bath willingly?" Billy asked in awe.

"How often do you bathe?"

"Only when Captain threatens he'll thrash me alive if I don't get meself clean."

Susan laughed. "I should hope he would. I thought it was myself whom I could smell; perhaps it's you?"

"I had a soaking the week afore we picked you up," Billy answered with a grin.

"In that case it most certainly must be me," Susan said. "I shall get to work straight away."

Billy remained at one side of the screen in case Susan felt ill. He chattered while she tried to get rid of several days' worth of grime. Her dress was badly crumpled and torn, but there was nothing she could do about her clothing. She could secure the tear under her petticoat sleeve, and although it looked odd, it maintained her dignity. The water was a shameful colour when she'd finished, but her skin was red with scrubbing. At least she felt slightly better for that.

Unwilling to climb back into bed, she was forced to sit quietly for a while in the cabin as the exertion had tired her. When Billy had cleared everything away, he brought her some luncheon, setting it down on the table.

"This is a lot of food," Susan said, eyeing the mounds of bread, cheese, ham and eggs.

"Lord Longdon said he'll join you," Billy said. "I've to go on deck and do some work. Captain says I've 'ad it easy too long."

"I think you've done a wonderful job in looking after me, and it can't have been easy."

Billy smiled. "It wasn't too bad. You don't give punches as oft as the captain does."

"Little rascal" Susan chided gently.

"What's the rapscallion doing now?" Miles asked as he ducked into the room.

"Absolutely nothing. He's a wonderful boy," Susan said.

Billy smiled from ear to ear, and with blushing cheeks he left the room.

"You've got an admirer there," Miles teased.

"I'm vastly in his debt," Susan said. "He kept it a secret that I'd awakened for as long as he possibly could. Then he was punished for trying to defend me."

"Yes, the bruise on his jaw is an impressive testament to that."

"It's cruel what he goes through. He doesn't moan or repine, just accepts it as a fact of his life," Susan said, nibbling on some cheese. "I don't suppose – it's only a thought, but could we take him with us when we dock?"

Miles blinked. "He'll be apprenticed to the captain."

"Surely there will be an amount of money that would release him?" Susan asked. "I'd be happy to pay it, if you could loan me the amount until I can reach a bank."

"And what happens to him when we free him?" Miles asked.

"He could come and work for me?"

71

"You don't have an establishment, and I can't see your father or stepmother being too happy at his arrival," Miles pointed out.

"Perhaps not. He could come and work for you?" Susan made an attempt at a winning smile, which because of her weakened state was quite wan, but all the more endearing for it.

"You free him, yet I am lumbered with an extra member of staff?" Miles asked archly.

"I'm sure there is some member of staff who would appreciate an extra pair of hands," Susan said, warming to her theme. "Someone who wouldn't beat him if he made a mistake."

"I don't overwork my staff, nor do I encourage the beating of my servants, Miss King," Miles said with a humph.

"Oh, no! Of course you don't, but he'd need someone who could nurture him, for he has a lot of potential. He just needs a little patience."

"The captain might be unwilling to release him, and you could be subjecting another child to the same treatment that Billy has had when they appoint another apprentice, for I'm sure they will," Miles reasoned.

"That's no reason to make a boy stay in a situation in which he is clearly unhappy. He has such a kind heart; he shouldn't be on a ship with a set of rogues. I'm sure you can persuade the captain to do as you wish, and give him a lecture on how he should treat those who are in his care."

"I'd like to point out that it's as *you* would wish, not I. Shouldn't you be the one to speak to the captain?" Miles asked dryly. He was entertained and charmed by Susan's passion for the injustice Billy had suffered through no fault of his own.

"No. He wouldn't listen to me. And you couldn't in all conscience leave a poor child to his fate. I can't believe you would be so cruel. Would you?"

"It doesn't look like I have any choice in the matter."

"Wonderful!" Susan exclaimed. "I knew I could rely on you. I'm sure it's for the best."

"Would you like to have a look over all the other sailors on board, in case you wish to adopt any of those?" Miles asked. He had the strangest feeling that if she came out with a list of names, he would find it hard to refuse her request.

"Now you are being foolish! You are teasing a woman who's in a sorry state. Shame on you, my lord."

"From my perspective, there's nothing wrong with you," Miles muttered.

"I confess I feel a lot better to know Billy's future will be brighter," Susan admitted. She was elated that her appeal to Miles was being taken seriously, something she was not used to. Her family had always dismissed anything she said.

"You have no doubt that I'll succeed?" Miles asked.

"Of course not. You are known for being able in whatever you embark on, and your fellow officers obviously look to you for direction. I therefore have every faith in your ability to persuade the captain to release Billy, no matter how much he argues against you. I know you won't let Billy down – you didn't fail me. You are the best of men."

"Your words are a little overwhelming," Miles said meekly.

"But true," Susan responded, her cheeks tinged with a blush at her admission of just some of her feelings about him.

Chapter 8

Susan was happy to be escorted out of the cabin on the third day. She was still easily tired but was determined to get some fresh air.

Jones and Dunn welcomed Susan as if she'd been their friend for years. Solicitations were exchanged, and they fussed around her, about where she could sit and if she was comfortable enough and out of the wind. They placed a blanket behind her and another over her knees, ensuring she would not be adversely affected by her venture out of doors.

"Leave the poor girl alone," Miles drawled at them.

"We don't want her catching a chill after going through so much," Dunn said defensively. "You might be an unfeeling brute, but we are gentlemen."

Miles shook his head. "If you're the best society can offer, God help us."

"Miss King, I hope you see how dastardly our friend serves us. If we don't retort, you may get a false impression of us, but if we *do* respond, then we risk the accusation of speaking in a coarse manner in front of a lady," Jones said.

Susan laughed. "Please don't hold back on my account," she said. "I think his lordship deserves everything he gets for being so wicked towards his friends."

"The three of you are perfectly matched," Miles said with a shrug. "I shall leave you to enjoy each other's company."

He walked away from the group. Dunn smiled at his retreating form. "He knows we hold him in high esteem really."

"I'm sure he does. I value you all. You have done me the best of services," Susan said a little shyly.

"It was our pleasure," Dunn replied. His words were sincerely meant. She was genuinely nice, unaffected and it had brought out the protective streak in them all.

"Yes, whenever you need rescuing, just let us know," Jones said. "We shall be there in a trice."

"I hope to have a far less eventful time in the future," Susan responded.

"If you should ever tire of the tedium that you are condemning yourself to, know that we're here for you," Jones said. "Daily life can be so utterly wearisome now we're at peace. It's nice to have an adventure occasionally."

"You'd much rather be at war? For that sounds to be the only type of escapade that appeals to you. Surely not?" Susan asked. Her rescuers fascinated her, partly because through them she gained more of an insight into Miles's life

"Oh yes," Jones said. "There's nothing quite like a battle to focus one's mind and make one feel really alive."

"My friend speaks nothing but bunkum," Dunn said at Susan's awed expression.

"I would think being in a battle would be terrifying," she said.

"One just has to get on with it at the time. It's afterwards that the reality of what you've faced hits you," Dunn admitted. "No sane person could enjoy it."

"Yet, you are all perfectly normal. Well, perhaps not Captain Jones so much," Susan said with a teasing smile.

Dunn burst out laughing, while Jones tried to look offended, but his eyes were twinkling at Susan. Smiling at them both, Susan didn't notice Miles's return.

"Longdon, your ward is a delight," Dunn said. "She's just put Jones in his place."

"That is a feat indeed," Miles said, smiling down at Susan.

"I was teasing, as Captain Jones is fully aware."

"You can make sport of me any day you wish," Jones said gallantly.

"You smooth devil," Miles mocked.

"One of us has to be," Jones responded, unperturbed.

"Are you ever serious?" Susan asked him. Enjoying the banter the men shared but being slightly intimidated by it at the same time.

"Not if I can possibly help it," Jones said. "Now, Longdon, are you going to share one of those fine cigars you have on your person? I've run out, and I'm loath to return to snuff."

Miles handed his friend a cigar out of the silver case he always carried, and Jones moved off to enjoy his smoke in peace. Sitting in the spot his friend had just vacated, Miles looked out over the sea. "I didn't think I'd be sailing again for a long time."

"Our friend has a tendency towards seasickness," Dunn supplied.

"Really? But you've travelled so far," Susan said to Miles.

Miles grimaced. "Unfortunately, experiencing any number of rough seas doesn't help. I'm usually fine on still waters."

"Then you've done me an even bigger service," Susan said with gratitude.

"You are going to turn into a real trump, aren't you, my good fellow?" Dunn asked Miles.

"On that note, I think I should return you to your cabin, Miss King. We don't want you to be overtired," Miles said, completely ignoring Dunn.

"If I must," Susan said. "Thank you for your company, Captain Dunn." She stood and accepted Miles's arm, and he walked her slowly back to her room.

*

Susan was keen to return out of doors the following morning and, with Billy's help, was soon seated in the sheltered spot she'd occupied the previous day. It was clear the sailors had been given strict instructions about any interactions with the young woman they were conveying, because although one or two surreptitious looks were aimed in her direction, she wasn't approached by anyone.

Miles smiled when he came above decks. "Enjoying the fine weather?" he asked pleasantly, coming to sit next to her.

"Yes. I've never been on any sea. It makes one feel quite small, doesn't it?" Susan said in wonder while gazing over the water.

"Travelling over to America certainly did that," Miles agreed. "Knowing you are days away from land is certainly a sobering thought as the ship creaks and groans through the night."

"Not a pleasant consideration for someone suffering from sickness either."

"No. Thanks to my friends, I'll soon have no secrets."

77

"They are both very amusing. And handsome, of course," Susan said.

"And don't they both know it!" Miles said. "They've broken a few hearts in their time."

"I'm sure you all have," Susan responded, a tinge of a blush on her cheeks.

Miles laughed. "Not at all. I was too focused on getting the job done to be distracted by anything else. Being attached to someone made you vulnerable."

"I never thought of it like that. I would have presumed it gave you strength," Susan said.

"Everyone has their own ways of coping, I suppose. Even you, who lives with a difficult relation, will have found ways to offset trouble. I know I do."

This time it was Susan's turn to smile. "Edith's ears probably wished to permanently close on some of the days I moaned into them."

"I'm sure you performed the same service in return. I know my own mother well enough to realise Edith will have been thoroughly distracted with Mama sometimes."

"She was a little, on occasion," Susan admitted. "It must be difficult for our parents, though. It was reasonable that any parent would expect us to marry in our first or second season. Especially with the fortune we both bring. Unfortunately neither of us seemed to take at all."

"You are very harsh on yourself. I know I am her brother, but I do see Edith's advantages. I also see her faults. All too clearly sometimes." Miles grimaced. "Especially when she decided to write that letter to the *Times*." He referred to the advertisement Edith had placed in the newspaper in order to find the type of beau she had struggled to find in society.

"Yes. It was a bold scheme."

"Did you know about it before she sent her letter in?" Miles asked.

"Me? No. Not at all. She only came to me when she received the first of the letters that turned out to be from Lord Pensby."

"I didn't think you would have encouraged her," Miles said, inordinately relieved that Susan had had nothing to do with the foolish scheme.

"No. I haven't the imagination, nor the daring," Susan admitted regretfully. She was pleased at Miles's words, but she had to be honest with him about her own character. Even if it put her to the disadvantage.

"In my opinion that's a distinct advantage."

"It makes me a poor, spiritless specimen," Susan said. "I disgust even myself with my lack of a backbone to embark on something as adventurous as Edith did. She decided to take her future into her own hands and find someone she wanted to spend the rest of her life with. Not many would have the daring or the resource to do what she did."

"You have experienced far more danger, injury and uncertainty than she ever has, and you've borne it all with fortitude. Don't put yourself down in favour of Edith. I can't allow it. I truly applaud the way you have dealt with this whole situation from the start," Miles said, genuinely wanting to convince her of his high regard.

"There was no point in becoming hysterical as events unfolded, for it wouldn't have changed anything," Susan said. "But I admit that I was afraid."

"It would have been odd for you not to be." Miles gently squeezed Susan's hand in reassurance. "We'll soon be at the mouth of the Thames. We should be docked by tomorrow afternoon, according to the captain."

"And then …"

"We return you to your aunt as you requested, but I suggest you have a letter written so we can send it to your father as soon as we dock," Miles said.

"The kidnap feels a little unreal now. If I didn't see the bloodstain from Mr. Malone's body on the floor of the cabin every time I move, I could almost convince myself none of it happened," Susan said.

"Pretending all is well is a good way of dealing with any situation you'd rather forget."

"Said by a seasoned campaigner," Dunn said, approaching the pair.

"Yes," Miles said.

Susan noticed that Miles's lips were set into a thin line but chose not to probe any further. "If you gentlemen would excuse me, I think I'll return to my cabin," she said, standing.

"I shall accompany you," Miles immediately offered.

"No. Stay here – it's such a nice sheltered spot. I'm feeling a little tired, but hopefully I'll return after having a short rest." The wind whipped her hair, which was barely fastened in place.

"Miss King, you look like a mermaid rising through the waves with your hair flying around you like that," Dunn said, much struck.

"Mermaids are supposed to be beautiful. Perhaps I'm half mermaid, half frightful beast?" Not waiting for a response, Susan waved her goodbye to the gentlemen and left them seated on the bench.

"I'd accuse her of false modesty, but she said that so unaffectedly, I actually think she believes it," Dunn said in some surprise.

Miles had watched Susan's retreat with a slight frown on his face. "I think you're right."

"She's not the prettiest girl I've ever seen, but she's no ape leader," Dunn said.

"No. Not at all," Miles agreed. "One would think she would be assured of her place in the world, but from a brief meeting with her parents, I feel there is a complicated family dynamic that has damaged the way she views herself."

"There's another dynamic that you seem to be oblivious to." Dunn gave his friend a half-smile.

"What's that?"

"The chit is smitten with you."

"Don't be ridiculous!"

"I'm not!" Dunn said, holding his hands up. "I see the way she gazes at you. I'd be more than happy to have anyone gazing at me that way."

"I'm too damaged to encourage anyone's affection," Miles admitted aloud for the first time.

"We all are, my friend," Dunn said gently. "We can only hope that the love of a good woman can help us continue to pretend we're living a normal life and haven't experienced the horrors we have. Those are ours to be haunted by until we find relief when we breathe our last. In the meantime, I have to find someone who can overlook the scarred mess that is my face, and you have to find someone who can chase the night terrors away. I presume you still suffer from them? I know you try to hide them from everyone, but I've heard them in the past."

Miles paused, upset that his friend knew of his weakness, but then nodded. "Yes. Which is one of the reasons why I'll remain single."

"A shame. For it's half the battle if they adore you to start with. More inclined to be understanding to our faults,"

Dunn said, standing. "I'll go and annoy the captain for a while. He does so amuse me with his tales of pirating."

Miles looked out over the horizon. The sky was grey and murky, although the sea was relatively calm; he expected that by nightfall there would be some sort of storm. At least by that time, they'd be on the Thames and have the protection the estuary would give.

He had caught Susan watching him a few times. Could it be something other than gratitude she felt? He'd always considered her as just his sister's friend. For the first time, he viewed her as a woman; it unsettled him a little, for he was astute enough to realise he was drawn to her. What had changed between them, he had no idea, but he knew she was becoming more important to him. A pity, then, he would have to dampen down such foolish emotions. He was too damaged.

*

Miles approached Susan. She was seated on the deck, tucked out of the way as she had been on her first venture outside. Her hope to return out of her cabin later in the afternoon of the previous day had been dashed by the weather, as Miles had predicted.

They were taking advantage of the increased wind and racing down the Thames, all sails filled with the wind as the boat raced across the top of the water. Susan watched the sails, the men working them, and the hustle and bustle around with avid interest, getting the most out of being on a ship in motion.

As he sat next to her, a smile played on his lips. "What schemes are you plotting? I can almost see the cogs turning as you watch everything."

Smiling in return, Susan moved to enable Miles to sit comfortably in the sheltered space. "I find the whole experience fascinating. This part of it, I hope you understand. Not the journey out," she clarified quickly.

"Of course. I understand," Miles said softly.

"I've barely travelled anywhere before, and never aboard a ship. I can't be thankful for what happened, but I shall treasure today at least as a wonderful memory."

"It's good to take the small positives from a situation we'd have rather not faced."

"You must have done that a lot," Susan probed gently.

"Yes."

Susan thought he wasn't going to say anything else, but after a moment or two, Miles spoke once more.

"I think the greatest shock is when you return home, having witnessed all kinds of horrors, and yet … yet life has gone on as normal whilst you've been away. It's sometimes hard to accept that someone who hasn't been there just can't appreciate what it was like."

"You could always try to explain."

"No. That would be unfair. Why try to make everyone as miserable as we are?" Miles asked with a rueful smile. "I'm prone to melancholy these days, Miss King. You can curse me to the devil if you will."

"Not at all. Your battles are a part of your life," Susan said. "It would be very poor of me to wish for you not to speak of them."

"Thank you, but for both our sakes, we should talk of something else. Tell me about your aunt," Miles encouraged, turning the conversation away from himself. He didn't want to see the pity in her eyes that would come if he explained his inner feelings about what he'd experienced.

"Aunt Florence? She's formidable." Susan smiled, accepting the change of subject. "She's been the best of relations since Papa remarried. My stepmother and I … Well, let's just say I'm not likeable to those to whom I'm not related."

Miles looked sharply at Susan. "That I cannot agree with."

"Oh, I'm not asking for false flattery," Susan said quickly. "Please don't presume I am, but my stepmother hasn't taken to me, just as I didn't take to her. We are both at fault. Aunt Florence wanted me to live with her, and I'd happily have done so, but Papa wouldn't hear of it. Probably the only time he ever stood up to Aunt Florence, that I can remember, anyway." She smiled. "As things turned out, it was a pity that Aunt Florence didn't get her own way like she usually does. I think we'd all have been happier."

"Was living at home so bad?" Miles couldn't resist asking.

"Not all the time," Susan admitted. "I have tried to keep out of my stepmother's way as much as possible. I pity her these last few years since my coming-out. We have been forced to spend a lot of time together during the season. I think that was one of her reasons for persuading Papa that I was to wed this season or they'd choose a husband for me."

"A hard decision to accept. I know Edith railed against my own mother when she suggested a potential suitor whom Edith didn't like."

"Yes. I'd planned to set up home with your sister, in a foolish, unrealistic scheme, but she foiled it by marrying a decent, lovely man!" Susan laughed gently.

"Very inconsiderate of her."

"Yes. Isn't it just?" Susan agreed. "Never mind. I shall throw myself at Aunt Florence's mercy, and I'm sure she'll have a plan for what to do for the best."

Chapter 9

"You have to marry! And soon!" Aunt Florence commanded within the first few moments of seeing her niece.

Susan had been escorted to her aunt's door by the three captains, after they had dropped Billy off at Miles's home. Handing Billy over to his butler would hopefully not frighten the boy, for the butler had looked in disdain at the child wrapped in rags who was put into his care. Miles had instructed the butler to go gently on the boy, but as he wished to escort Susan and ensure she was well settled with her aunt, it would be some time before he returned to sort out Billy's future.

Miles had almost blushed as Susan had clasped his hands when Billy was released to come with them, his few belongings wrapped into a bundle.

"Oh, you did it! I knew you would!" she'd cried out to Miles. "Billy, you'll have a far better future serving his lordship. He doesn't beat his staff, so you need have no fear on that score."

"You'll have me known as a soft touch," Miles had complained, not pulling his hands from her gentle hold.

"Not at all. It is a generous and kind thing you have done," Susan responded.

Miles thought it prudent not to look at the expressions on his friends' faces, which were incredulous and amused in equal measure. Instead he encouraged Susan down the gangway and into a hired carriage.

Jones and Dunn had bowed over her hand and sent their best wishes for her continued safety as soon as they'd reached Susan's aunt's home. They'd expressed the desire to return to their barracks and make themselves presentable before appearing in public. Miles had remained with her even in his dishevelled state, wishing to know her aunt would offer the protection Susan was convinced she would give.

Knocking on Aunt Florence's door after saying their goodbyes to Jones and Dunn, Susan had looked at Miles, for the first time a little nervous. "I wonder what Papa has told her?"

"Don't worry about that now. We'll soon tell her what really happened," Miles had assured her.

They were ushered into the drawing room and were not long alone. Susan's aunt hurried through the door to greet her unexpected guests.

She was a large woman, in height and width, one described by acquaintances quite appropriately as bustling. She came into the room, wearing a dress of deep red, with more flounces and frills than was usual on a lady of her advanced years. A large feathered turban gave her even more height. She seemed to fill the room she'd just entered. Miles could perfectly understand why Mr. King was intimidated by his sister; in dress alone she was something to behold.

"Oh, my dear child!" she exclaimed, wrapping her niece in a warm embrace. "Are you married?"

"No, Aunt. It was a forced kidnap and elopement, which, thankfully, Lord Longdon and his friends foiled," Susan explained briefly.

"Oh dear," Florence replied, sitting heavily onto the nearest sofa.

"Aunt, surely it's good news that I was rescued?" Susan was astounded at the response she was receiving.

That was when she uttered the unbelievable words. "You have to marry! And soon!"

"What?" Susan asked, herself sinking onto a chair.

"I think we need to have this conversation in private." Florence looked at Miles. "I thank you for the safe return of my niece, but we have urgent matters to discuss."

"I'd rather Lord Longdon remained, if you've no objections, my lord? I'd value your opinion in yet another trying situation, though I realise I'm asking even more of you." Susan knew she was being unfair, but she couldn't help it. She needed his support.

"I shall do my utmost to assist," Miles said seriously.

"Thank you. Again."

"It's that blasted stepmother of yours," Florence cursed. "She's spread it around town that you've eloped. They've said they don't know who you've eloped with, but they are prepared to welcome him into the family because you've always wanted to be part of a romantic escapade."

"Who, knowing me, would believe that tale of folly? Why would she spread such a story? She's ruined me," Susan whispered, sagging against the cushions as she realised the implications of her stepmother's actions. "I thought the danger was from Mr. Sage, but it was from my own family as well. How am I to overcome this?"

"If you don't return married, you most certainly will be ruined," Florence said. "The only thing you could do is establish yourself somewhere as far away from London and polite society as you could get. I'm sorry, child. I wouldn't wish this fate on you my most precious niece, but these are cards you've been dealt. I will obviously accompany you."

"No, no, no!" Susan said. "Why should your social life be curtailed because my father married a harridan?"

Florence laughed bitterly. "She's that, all right. But this situation is serious, I'm afraid, Susan. You can't return unmarried."

"I must leave town. Immediately," Susan said. "But I refuse your offer of escort, Aunt."

"I would suggest you don't embark on a long journey," Miles interjected. "You are only just recovering from a fever, and your arm still pains you."

"How do you know it still hurts?" Susan asked, diverted from her present trouble.

"The way you hold it and favour your other arm whenever possible. It doesn't take much intelligence to work out that you are suffering, but doing it without complaint," Miles explained.

"I thought I was disguising it well."

Miles smiled at her. "Not well enough."

Florence interrupted the pair. "I think you'd better tell me everything that happened."

Susan went through the whole story, even confessing that she'd written to Miles for help. When she finished, she sat back. "I'm at a loss as to why my mother chose to make the kidnap public, albeit her version of events."

"You said she was determined to marry you this season," Miles said quietly.

"Yes, and this way she's guaranteed I either return married and I'm off her hands, or I'm unable to return at all, which achieves the same outcome." There was no self-pity in Susan's tone; her words were said matter-of-factly.

89

"I told my brother he'd picked a woman who hadn't a maternal bone in her body when he expressed a desire to marry her. He should have found someone who could give you a mother's love, not someone as fickle and vain as she is. There was never a person on this earth she loved, apart from herself, of course," Florence said.

"What about her own son? She loves him," Susan said of her half-brother.

"He was sent away to school as soon as he could walk. It was only because he ailed that your father insisted he be schooled at home. She hasn't got a heart; she'd have left him at school to take his chances there. My brother is as stupid as a greenhorn. I'm heartily ashamed to acknowledge we are blood related!"

Florence's rant was interrupted by the butler. "Madam, there is a Captain Dunn wishing to speak to Lord Longdon as a matter of urgency."

Miles rose. "Might I speak to him somewhere private?" he asked Florence. He wasn't as yet ready to abandon Susan whilst there was so much uncertainty about her future, although in reality there was little he could offer in the way of help.

"Of course. Use the morning room," Florence said.

"Please excuse me." Miles bowed before leaving the room.

Seeing Dunn standing agitatedly in the hallway, Miles nodded in his direction, and both men followed the butler to the small room at the rear of the property. It was about half the size of the drawing room, but equally as grand.

When the butler left the men in private, Miles turned to his friend. "What is it?" he asked without preamble. There was obviously something amiss to have caused Dunn's sudden appearance and his discomfited expression.

"We're in a real pickle this time, Longdon!" Dunn said.

"What can have possibly gone wrong now? You only left me an hour ago, if not less."

"One of us has to marry Miss King," Dunn blurted out.

"What?"

"You heard me!" Dunn snapped. "It seems our disappearance and hers have been linked. There's a wager in White's as to who has secured the runaway heiress. I was bombarded with questions the moment I entered the blasted place! I tell you, it took all the guile I've picked up from Jones to get myself out of there without letting on what had actually happened."

"Damn that blasted woman!" Miles cursed.

"Miss King?" Dunn asked in surprise.

"No. Her stepmother. She's concocted some Banbury story that her daughter had eloped with her lover as a ploy for a romantic marriage. If Susan isn't married, she's ruined."

"That's not quite right. If she isn't married *to one of us*, she's ruined," Dunn pointed out. He felt a cad but his words were necessary.

"We could surely explain that away?" Miles said. "There's only a presumption the two disappearances are linked."

"You know the way gossip clings to a person. They've linked us with Miss King through you."

"That's ludicrous! We could have gone out of town for any number of reasons."

"Yes, but most of those reasons don't include a hurried exit without our valets," Dunn pointed out. "Nor did we cancel the engagements we'd accepted. Actions like those are remarked on. Our motivation was rightly about speed, but we should have been more circumspect. People know of your hurried return to the city and your equally as quick departure. Your mother has been repining the fact she didn't have the opportunity to see you."

"The devil take it! Why are we surrounded by interfering, unthinking relatives!" Miles said heatedly. "It's going to require some serious thinking to get out of this one."

"It seems perfectly straightforward to me," Dunn replied.

"Does it?"

"Yes. You've got to wed the girl. And soon."

Chapter 10

Miles sat down. Hard. "I can't do that," he croaked out.

"Why not? You know her. She's a fine woman, pleasant, attractive. Neither Jones nor I have any intention of marrying anytime soon, but as head of your family you need an heir. It makes a lot of sense." Dunn shrugged.

"But marriage?" Miles asked, still in shock.

"Yes. We can't let her be ruined, can we? She's worth more than that. She's besotted with you, which isn't a bad start to wedded bliss, and you must at least like her," Dunn cajoled.

"She's my sister's friend. I have no objection to her as such, she's very nice, but to spend the rest of my life with her? That's something completely different." Miles paled.

"You clearly regard her more than you realise, or why the dash across country when she was in trouble?"

"It was the right thing to do," Miles said weakly.

"And so is this," Dunn pointed out. "Would it be so bad?"

"I hadn't intended marrying for years," Miles said. "What am I saying? I didn't want to marry at all." He had once thought he would wed and have many children, but that was a dream without the reality of showing someone else how the war had affected him.

"Why not? You've spent enough time in my company to be charming, and you're a relatively handsome chap in the right light."

Miles's lips twitched, before he became serious once more. "I'm too damaged."

"We all are," Dunn admitted. "And I don't just refer to the ones who were away fighting."

"But we're more mangled than most. I don't want to inflict that on anyone, least of all a wife who's being forced to marry me because of circumstance."

"As the head of the family, you have obligations, and the moment you responded to Miss King's appeal for help, you became obligated to her. This solution solves both issues in one fell swoop," Dunn said.

Miles roughly rubbed a hand over his face. "I didn't think marriage would be a consequence of helping her," he said. "I couldn't leave her feeling unsafe with Malone around, but this, this is something else."

"It's not too bad, is it?" Dunn asked. "I think she'd make a good wife."

"You marry her, then," Miles said.

"She's besotted with you. We all want a mate who adores us – you've got that before you even start."

"I need to think," Miles said. He seemed to Dunn to be in shock.

"I'll leave you be, but don't dwell too long. That girl needs to be wed with a special licence," Dunn cautioned.

Miles nodded slightly, but Dunn wasn't sure his friend had registered his words. Feeling that he could do no more, he left Miles to ponder his future.

*

It was over half an hour before Miles returned to the drawing room. As soon as he entered, Susan went to him in concern.

"My lord, what has happened? You are deathly pale," she cried.

Miles focused on her. "It seems we are in more of a fix than we first thought," he said, his voice quieter than normal.

"Come. Sit and tell me what's amiss," Susan said, guiding him to a chair.

"You'd better explain to us what's happened, young man," Florence demanded.

"My friend informs me that our joint disappearances have been linked, and there is, umm, some speculation on who has married you. One of the three of us has been identified as the husband you shall be returning with," Miles said dully.

"Good God!" Susan said, horrified. "Will this nightmare ever end?"

Miles glanced at her with some sympathy. "Yes. It appears we need to marry."

"What? No!" Susan exclaimed, standing agitatedly and walking away from Miles.

"Am I that repulsive?" Miles asked. A small smile played at his lips despite his own opinions on the situation.

"You know very well you aren't. Anyone would be lucky to have you as their husband," Susan responded primly. "But I refuse to let you be a sacrificial lamb on my account."

Florence gave the pair an appraising look before speaking. "It would solve your problems," she said to her niece.

"And create a whole lot more for myself, but even more for Lord Longdon. No. I shall remove myself from London," Susan said, her tone firm.

Miles sighed. Having resigned himself to the inevitable, he now had to convince Susan it was the only option they had. "Where could you go that you wouldn't ever see anyone who knew you, or knew your story?"

"One of the remote islands of Scotland?" Susan asked hopefully.

"And each summer, travellers looking for the next picturesque viewpoint, mountain or village would descend. You'd be in a constant state of fear of being exposed as the woman who eloped with three men and came back unwed," Florence pointed out.

"It isn't fair! Lord Longdon only came to my aid because I wrote to him. Why should he have to sacrifice himself by marrying me?" Susan cried. She was mortified that the man she loved would be forced into marriage with her in such a way. It didn't matter that it was her deepest wish. This way was an underhand method of gaining the husband she longed for.

"You speak as if you are some sort of waspish mopsey. And she is nothing of the sort," Florence said, aiming her last words towards Miles.

"I am well aware of that," Miles acknowledged.

"You bring with you a lot of advantages to a marriage, even without your fortune," Florence pointed out to Susan.

"And that is why I'm unmarried at three and twenty," Susan said dryly. "Oh, this is too much! I won't accept your more than generous offer, my lord. This is my problem and mine alone."

"I'm afraid when a bet is set up in White's about my future, it is no longer purely about you," Miles said.

"Oh, dear Lord!" Florence said. "They're taking bets on who's married her?"

"It would appear so, madam," Miles responded. "Dunn thought it prudent to warn us before anyone realised we'd all returned without one of us being wed to your niece. Apparently he was accosted as soon as he entered White's, but he didn't reveal anything."

Susan sat down, all fight and indignation gone. "This wouldn't have happened if my stepmother hadn't spread her vicious tale."

"No," Miles said gently. He moved across to Susan, automatically responding to her distress. "This is a situation not of our making, but we have the means to make the best of it. I'll get us a special licence, and we'll marry in the morning. We can send a message to the *Times* and say we were recently married. No one needs to know the exact date."

"But you don't want to marry me!" Susan's cheeks flushed in mortification.

"I didn't want to marry anyone," Miles said, his voice soft. "We rub along, don't we? That's not a bad start to a marriage. I won't ill-treat you, that I promise."

"I know you wouldn't," Susan said quietly, not able to meet Miles's eyes. "That's not the point though, is it?"

Miles took Susan's hand and squeezed it reassuringly. "There isn't an alternative."

"I'm sorry." Tears swam in Susan's eyes as she finally looked at Miles. "I am so sorry."

Kissing Susan's hand, Miles smiled at her. "We'll muddle through. I shall leave you now and obtain a licence. I'll send word round as to where you need to be in the morning. We can return to my home on Curzon Street after the ceremony and send out the notifications to introduce ourselves as a married couple. We can say we've had a long-lasting romance, only we kept it a secret. I wanted to make the most romantic gesture and whisked you away to be married. It might be scoffed at initially, but if we pretend to be in love, they'll start to believe it."

Susan nodded, unable to speak. Standing, Miles bowed to Florence.

"I'll send a missive round later to advise on what I've achieved. I shall be keeping a low profile and won't be out in company this evening."

"That's wisest," Florence agreed. "We shall await your instructions."

With one last sympathetic glance at Susan, Miles left the room, leaving the two women staring at each other.

"There won't be any pretence in your acting as if you're in love with him, will there?" Florence asked gently.

"No."

"My dear, look at it this way. You are marrying the man you love, and your combined wealth will have your stepmother seething with jealousy."

Susan wrung her hands without speaking. The points her aunt had raised offered no comfort to her.

*

Dunn approached Jones in White's "Have you arranged it?"

"Of course? Did you doubt my ability?" Jones drawled.

"Setting up a bet without anyone knowing it was us who started it isn't easy," Dunn pointed out.

98

"No. But then not everyone has my talents," Jones replied.

"Or vanity."

"As I've done this for the benefit of our friend, I would like to think of it as a selfless act of friendship," Jones said. He was convinced it was the right course of action to have taken.

"I don't think he's too happy at the moment. I left him looking part put out, part shocked," Dunn said.

"Perhaps for now, but he doesn't recognise his own attachment," Jones explained patiently. "Miss King's eyes might have followed our good friend around wherever he went, but he was equally as watchful of her."

"To be fair to him, she'd been ill. I admit I watched her more than I would any other female," Dunn said.

"Your expression didn't have a mix of longing and wistfulness about it," Jones said. "There's a difference in his behaviour to that of a man who is helping his sister's friend. He is in love with the chit; he just doesn't realise it. We needed to give him a little push."

"If he ever finds out, he'll kill us," Dunn warned.

"Hopefully he won't until he acknowledges his own emotions. Otherwise it'll be a dash to the Continent for us both," Jones said with a confident smile.

Chapter 11

Susan could barely look at Miles as they said their vows in the small chapel a few streets away from where Florence lived. They'd travelled there in a hired hackney carriage, unwilling to have their own carriages seen in the vicinity. The only other persons attending were Jones, Dunn and Florence.

She wore a dress hastily altered from her aunt's wardrobe. Luckily for Florence's lady's maid, she didn't have to stay up all night sewing. Susan and Florence had sat with her and sewn until their fingers hurt the evening before the wedding, thus enabling Susan to wear a dress wholly fitting for her wedding day. The dress she'd worn since the kidnap was falling apart, and her petticoat had hung around her knees since being hacked to provide bandages for her arm.

With heightened colour and swirling emotions, Susan accepted the plain gold band on her finger, which Miles had somehow secured in less than a day. Her hands were shaking, which Miles responded to by keeping hold of her hand once he'd placed the ring on it. Susan looked up at his face and received a reassuring smile, although she was saddened to note that his eyes weren't smiling as they usually were.

The service was over very soon, and the bride and groom walked down the aisle together, joined forever. They received the congratulations of the three people who had witnessed the event, and then entered a hackney carriage, leaving their friends on the pavement to wave them off.

"What did you tell your mother when you returned home last night?" Susan asked when the carriage had turned the corner away from the church.

"I stayed with Jones," Miles admitted. "My mother can be imprudent sometimes, so I thought it best to present her with the deed already done."

"I can't apologise enough," Susan said again. "I don't think I'll ever stop feeling guilty."

"You can't keep saying things like that," Miles said. "We have to put on a united, believable show for anyone watching. You need to relax so that we can both carry this off. Otherwise it will have been for naught."

Susan grimaced. "Easier said than done."

"You are doing nothing for my ego," Miles teased gently.

Unable to prevent the chuckle escaping, Susan looked gratefully at Miles. "Thank you," she said quietly.

"You're welcome," Miles responded, unable to stop himself from responding to any distress Susan felt.

*

Lady Longdon was upstairs when the couple arrived in Curzon Street. Miles took Susan into the drawing room and ordered refreshments to be served and a message sent to his mother.

"I couldn't eat anything," Susan said as the door closed on the pair.

"I could," Miles answered. "Unless I get regular fixes of sustenance I turn into a bear, apparently."

"Noted for future reference," Susan replied archly.

"A perfect wife," Miles murmured before they were interrupted.

Lady Longdon entered the room in a flurry of frilly dressing gown and waving hands. "Miles! Where have you been?" She faltered when she saw Susan. Her eyes narrowed. "What are you doing here, Susan?"

"Mother, I know this will come as a little surprise, but Susan is your new daughter," Miles said, taking Susan's hand and squeezing it in support.

"I don't understand."

"I apologise for not telling you before the event, but I've held Susan in affection for many a year, and she's finally agreed to be my wife," Miles patiently explained. "We thought we'd have an adventure and eloped. You are the first person to greet us as man and wife."

"No! This can't be! You are one of the most wanted single men of the season!" Lady Longdon exclaimed.

Susan tried to pull away from Miles, but he held firm, only releasing her hand so he could wrap his arm around her middle and pull her towards him. "Mother, Susan is my wife, the new Lady Longdon, and I expect her to be greeted as would be warranted by her position in society and in this family," Miles said.

Lady Longdon paled at the threat in her son's words. "You could have done so much better. Susan, you are unobjectionable as a girl – in fact, I often thought you were a good influence on Edith – but I cannot accept this. You must have tricked my son somehow. He would never have looked at you otherwise."

"Mother!" Miles hissed.

Susan stood a little straighter. "I think you'll find he wanted my fortune," she said damningly. Moved by anger, she'd retorted with some asperity.

In one fluid movement, Miles swung Susan around so that she was facing him and, bending his head, he crushed his lips against hers. It was a kiss that was forceful, possessive and passionate, albeit short. Pulling away from Susan, Miles stared into her eyes.

"I wanted you as my wife. No other."

Susan blinked and nodded. She couldn't have spoken if she had needed to. To say Miles's actions and words had surprised her would be an understatement. She was stunned.

"Miles! Restrain yourself!" Lady Longdon scolded.

Miles smiled at Susan and moved away from her to give the bell pull at the side of the fireplace a tug.

The butler entered the room almost immediately.

"Ah good," Miles said. "Please have the staff prepared to greet the new Lady Longdon. My mother shall use the title Dowager from now on."

"Yes, m'lud," came the unfazed reply. "The staff shall be in the hallway within five minutes."

"Excellent." Miles smiled at Susan's horrified face. "You need to have formal introductions. Then I shall give instructions for your room to be set up. Mother, you will be sleeping in the blue chamber from now on. Once we've done the greetings, we can visit your parents. I thought it would be sensible to start here as we need to have rooms changed."

"I am to be usurped?" Lady Longdon asked. "What about Miss Robinson and Miss Webster? Are they to be sent away now you have returned?" Lady Longdon asked of her friends who had moved in when her son and daughter had left the capital.

"Of course they can stay. I'm sure neither of us would object to their remaining here, especially as our future plans aren't decided yet," Miles answered honestly.

"I could sleep in the blue chamber," Susan offered.

"No. You will sleep in the room designated for my wife," Miles said firmly.

"I don't wish to cause any trouble."

"You aren't causing any trouble." Miles directed a warning glance at his mother. "You are Lady Longdon. My wife. You shall have what's rightly due to your rank and position. Won't she, Mother?"

Lady Longdon looked to be battling internally, but eventually she nodded. "Of course she will."

"Good. That's settled, then. Come, my dear. Let's go and meet your servants."

Susan followed her husband meekly out of the door.

Finding Billy lined up with the rest of the servants turned Susan's mind to a more positive subject. "Oh, Billy! It's so good to see you! Have you settled in?"

"Yes, m'lady," Billy said with a bow.

The young man's actions brought a smile to Susan's lips. "And what job have you been assigned?"

"The boot-boy for now, m'lady," the butler said. He'd remained silent but didn't wish Billy's exuberance to overcome him.

"He's a hard worker," Susan said.

"He's very keen to please," the butler admitted. "He's being taught the differences between life on board and the work in a house."

"That's an excellent plan," Susan said.

"Thank you, m'lady."

"I'm glad to have you working for us, Billy," Susan said to the boy before moving on to the next servant.

Billy beamed, and before Susan was out of earshot, he whispered. "They don't cuss me, or hit me if I make a mistake!"

"Good." Susan smiled, whilst trying to stifle a giggle at the butler's stiffened response to the words. "The captain of the ship he belonged to wasn't a very nice man, very keen with his fists," she said quietly to assure the butler that Billy wasn't being disparaging towards his new household.

Receiving a nod of understanding, she continued to follow the introductions made by the butler, thankful that Billy was safe.

*

To say that Mrs. King was astounded that the disappearance of her stepdaughter would result in her returning having made a very eligible match was an understatement. Mr. King was delighted and embraced his daughter warmly.

"Oh, my dear, you are secure and I'm sure you will be happy! A lady! How wonderful for you to have a title to go with your inheritance," he gushed, before taking Miles's hand and pumping it enthusiastically. "Well done, my boy. Well done indeed. I am indebted to you – you promised my Susan's safe return and you've achieved it with some style."

Miles couldn't help smiling. "I suppose I did," he answered. "I'm glad you are pleased, and if we could retire to your study, we can discuss the finer details of the match."

"She'll get her fortune, don't you worry," Mr. King said.

"I wasn't considering that. I was going to discuss *my* wealth," Miles said with a bashful smile.

"You'll be as rich as Croesus!" Mr. King smiled at his daughter.

"Papa! Really," Susan said, but there was no censure in her tone. "It pleases me that you are happy with the match."

"We couldn't have done better if we'd planned the match ourselves, could we, m'dear?" Mr. King glanced at his wife. "We should throw a ball to celebrate."

"Oh no!" Susan said quickly. "Surely it won't be necessary? People will be curious about the circumstance of our marriage and be watching for any signs of scandal. I'd much rather just try to creep back into society."

"That is a sure way of admitting guilt, and although it was an adventure, it's turned out well," Miles pointed out with a smile. "Perhaps we could have a smaller celebration? It would seem odd if there wasn't some form of event to mark the occasion."

"Quite so," Mr. King agreed. "Let's retire to my study, my lord, and have a chat over a brandy. These two can start to plan what extravaganza they would like to arrange. We don't need to be here for the finer details."

Miles shot Susan a smile of encouragement before the two men left her alone with her stepmother.

A silence descended on the pair, which after a few minutes was finally broken by Susan. "I'd rather we just had a meal or a small gathering, if you wouldn't mind?"

"You don't wish to proclaim it from the housetops about your fortunate catch?"

"No. The whole escapade has left me feeling a little drained and very tired," Susan said. "I'd like a quiet life for the foreseeable future."

"Was it you who was injured? There was blood on the ground in the garden."

"I was shot in the arm," Susan said, rubbing the top of her left arm. "I was lucky that there was no connection to the bone, but it still hurts and caused a severe fever."

"You are lucky to come out of the whole escapade, then."

"Yes." Susan never knew whether there were any feelings behind her stepmother's words, always suspicious that her comments were barbed. Another uncomfortable silence descended.

"And who were your real captors?" Mrs King asked eventually.

"Mr. Malone and Mr. Sage."

"You could have married one of them."

"No! Their aim was to access my inheritance, and then I would have been no longer needed," Susan said, appalled.

"You have always had an overactive imagination," Mrs. King replied. "I'm sure you would have been perfectly safe."

"I beg pardon for disagreeing with you, Mama, but you didn't hear the things they were saying. It was terrifying."

"And so you were rescued by the honourable Lord Longdon," Mrs. King said, sounding bored.

"Yes. Not a second too soon. The clergyman was on board the ship." Susan shuddered.

"A convenient situation for you."

"I don't understand," Susan said. She was a married woman and yet she was still as intimidated by her stepmother as she always was. It would seem marriage wouldn't give her the courage to stand up to her parent.

"Once your kidnappers had been foiled, the clergyman was there to carry out a different wedding."

"Oh. I see. Yes, of course," Susan said quickly.

"And you both live happily ever after."

"I hope so. Doesn't everyone wish for that when they are married?"

"I suppose they do, but most of us have to be pragmatic and accept what we can," Mrs. King said.

"My father has given you everything you wished for!" Susan said, hotly defending her father.

"Maybe. Marriage can be tedious, as you will no doubt find out." Mrs. King looked at Susan appraisingly. "I have to bow to your success. I would never have aimed so high if I had your lack of looks and address. You really have done well for yourself considering the disadvantages you bring to a match."

Susan flushed a deep pink. "You speak as if I set out to marry Lord Longdon."

"Did you not? He admitted you'd written to him. Was it not some ploy to get yourself the husband you actually wanted?" Mrs. King asked.

"How could you think that I would be so deceitful? And why on earth would I arrange to be shot? A foolhardy scheme indeed!" She was mortified that the situation could be twisted in such a way and a flush of heat coursed through her body as she hoped that Miles didn't think the same.

Mrs. King shrugged. "You were barely hurt. You said so yourself."

"I had a raging fever for days!" Susan exclaimed.

"You are young and healthy. A reasonable assumption you'd recover. No, I have to admit you've done well. You've always been a pasty-faced, uninteresting little thing. I was convinced we would have to increase your fortune to get someone to take you off our hands. Bravo on your success!"

"Thankfully, my wife didn't need anything but her charms to tempt me into marrying her once I realised what a fool I'd been in not acknowledging my feelings for her," Miles said from the open doorway. His voice was as pleasant as always, but his expression was thunderous.

Susan expected her stepmother to look abashed, but Mrs. King hardly turned towards Miles. "Then she's even more fortunate than I first thought," she responded with a shrug.

"Fortunate that she has a title, a large property in the country and has doubled her wealth, for I am no pauper, madam," Miles said tersely. "You are mistaken that your daughter has been lucky in our match. It is I who is the lucky one."

"My lord, I—" Susan started.

"My dearest Susan, what do I keep telling you? Use my given name, for I am yours now as much as you are mine. We need no formalities." Miles crossed the room to Susan. "Come. Let us return home. We have done our duty. Your father is to arrange for your belongings and your maid to be sent to our house."

Susan followed Miles out of the room. Kissing her father, who had remained in the hallway, on the cheek, she said her goodbyes. She didn't speak to Miles until she was out of earshot of her father.

Susan turned haunted eyes towards Miles. "How much did you hear?"

"Enough to realise that you've been extremely patient with that woman over the years," Miles said grimly. "Why does she dislike you so much?"

"You noticed that?" Susan asked with a small smile. "I don't really know. Perhaps jealousy that my father dotes on me? For he does. Undeservedly so, for I have little to recommend myself, I know."

Narrowing his eyes, Miles looked at Susan. "I wish you wouldn't say things like that. I've only noticed it recently, and it isn't true. Everyone you meet likes you."

"Except my stepmother, Mr. Malone, Mr. Sage, and now your mother," Susan responded dryly.

"They don't count." Miles grinned. "Two are dead, and the other two will just have to put up with it."

"I never thought I'd say something as wicked as this, but I hope two of them are dead. We can be sure of only Mr. Malone's demise," Susan pointed out.

"Sage couldn't have survived in the mud. But enough of him. Don't accept any nonsense from my mother," Miles instructed. "I feel you've been too meek with your stepmother. You don't deserve such censure or disrespect, and I refuse to let you accept it as Lady Longdon. You have a title and position to uphold – don't let my mother or yours undermine you."

"I've been in the habit of assuming it is just the way I am and that she's right to criticise," Susan admitted. "And I say this not wishing to stir any sympathy, but when you are told that you are plain, uninteresting and have nothing of value to offer, it's only a certain amount of time before you start to believe it. A pitiful specimen, am I not?"

"To be pitied, perhaps, but not because of anything you did. I would hate to think Edith had been persecuted to such an extent," Miles said. It didn't rest easy with him that Susan had been treated so ill.

"Your words are too strong," Susan said. "I haven't been persecuted! There are people in far worse situations than I. Please don't think I repine, for I don't."

"Which is to your credit. If you have any further difficulties with either your mother or mine, you need to tell me immediately."

"I'm sure I won't have anything to complain about."

"I hope not, but just in case you do, remember that we are a couple now," Miles said. "We shall overcome problems together."

"Thank you."

Miles would never know how much his words meant to Susan. She hadn't thought she could love him more. It appeared she could.

Chapter 12

Susan sat on the edge of her bed in the room assigned for the lady of the house. Being a London house, there was only a small sitting room separating it from the main bedroom. A dressing room was beyond the opposite wall. Hers was a large room, with two wardrobes, a chest of drawers, a chaise longue, a desk and a large four-poster bed.

Having sat for half an hour staring at the bed, Susan had eventually plucked up the courage to move and sit on the edge of it.

It was her wedding night.

She was married to a man she'd been in love with for years.

Why, then, was she terrified of what was to come?

Twisting her nightgown until it was tightly wrapped around her fingers, she silently cursed herself. This was no good. She went to the fireplace and warmed her hands near the flames.

When she could delay it no longer, she approached the bed quickly and climbed under the blankets. Pulling the covers high around her shoulders, she sat for a while.

Eventually, she realised her husband wasn't going to visit her, and she lay down. Still watching the door that led into the sitting room, she eventually fell into a fitful sleep.

*

Miles had pondered long and hard about what to do on his wedding night. It would be easy to go to Susan: he liked her, and knowing she had feelings for him would make it easier to perform his duty as a new husband, but it felt wrong.

After two large glasses of port, he decided it was best to remain friends. For the first time he gave credit to what his sister had insisted on – being in love with the person she married. He was in a situation that wasn't of his choosing, but he was sure they could live together amicably. He nodded to his valet to prepare his nightwear.

A pity amicability wasn't love, but he wasn't in love with Susan, so there was no benefit in acting as if he were, except when they were in company. Then it would be important they both maintain the façade of being happily married.

After dismissing his valet, he blew his candle out and climbed into bed. Being friends would have to be enough.

*

Susan was relieved to find out that her mother-in-law didn't appear downstairs until morning calls started. Feeling a little on edge about seeing Miles was going to be bad enough without being scrutinised by a woman who hadn't shown any welcome towards her.

Blushing when Miles entered the dining room, she gave a tentative smile. "Good morning."

"Good morning, Susan. You might wish to write to Edith this morning. I've sent her an express about our situation as I've already sent the notice to the *Times*. You can tell her as much as you choose to; I shall leave it up to you how much you reveal," Miles said pleasantly.

113

"I'd like to tell her everything," Susan said. "We've never had secrets before now, so I wouldn't like to start."

"Edith will be discreet," Miles agreed.

"Yes," Susan replied. There was no doubt in Susan's mind of Edith's discretion as her friend hadn't revealed her secret when she'd confessed her feelings for Miles.

"Shall we have a quiet day today and start to accept invitations from tomorrow?"

"I think it would be wisest. Let people get over the shock of seeing the notice in the paper before we venture out."

"I'd like to take you to Barrowfoot House, but we would have to be away a while in order to travel there and back and spend a couple of days there," Miles mused. "It might seem strange if we were to leave London so soon, do you think?"

"No, I don't. I'd be happy to leave today. By the time we return, our story will be old news," Susan suggested. "We could class it as our wedding trip."

"That's a good idea." Miles smiled. "Do you feel well enough for the journey? It is only days since we couldn't consider travelling across the country with you in a carriage."

"I'll be fine," Susan assured him. "It isn't the same distance, and if we can take our time, the journey shouldn't be too tiresome."

"In that case, we'll set a relaxed pace," Miles said. "Shall we start out this afternoon?"

"Yes please." Then there would be less awkwardness between your mother and myself, Susan thought, but she didn't voice the words. She didn't wish either of them to be made more uncomfortable than they already were by their present situation.

114

Embarking on another journey so soon didn't necessarily appeal to Susan, but being out of public scrutiny did. She spent the morning writing a letter to Edith, once she'd instructed her maid on which dresses to pack. Her poor maid had only just settled into the room, and she was already refilling a portmanteau.

*

Susan had wondered about sleeping arrangements on the journey, as it would take two nights at a leisurely pace to travel to the family home, but Miles organised everything. Two rooms were obtained, and although he ensured they were next to each other, once they had said their goodnights, Susan was not disturbed by her husband.

Although she'd felt a faint sense of disappointment and relief the first night, after then there seemed to be a dead weight in the pit of her stomach. She didn't think it would go away any time soon. The thought of a wedding night in the truest sense of the word had worried her, but the fact that Miles hadn't come to her felt like a rejection. She was obviously not appealing enough to tempt him, no matter what platitudes he'd uttered as a result of her stepmother's scorn.

Entering the grounds of the Longdon homestead, Susan watched through the window as the carriage trundled along the driveway. A natural woodland had been allowed to form along the driveway, offering glimpses of further parkland through the trees. As the carriage continued the woodland ended and the space opened up to the sight of the house, surrounded by more formal grounds. It was an impressive, yet natural, way of viewing the house.

"Feel free to change anything in the house you would wish to," Miles said as the familiar views greeted him.

"You could live to regret saying that," Susan said with a smile.

"I trust you to alter what needs changing and improving as you see fit. You are not one to change things just for the sake of it."

"Hmm, I'm not sure I want to be considered so sensible and predictable," Susan mused, a glint in her eye.

"As I'd prefer that to my mother's excesses, believe me when I say it's a compliment."

As they came to a sweeping stop in front of the modern Palladian-style house, Susan sat back. "Another line of staff to greet."

"As they are your staff, enjoy their welcome," Miles encouraged.

"I wish I had more of your affable, sociable character. I'm far too inclined to be reticent."

"You are quietly friendly and welcoming. People respond well to you. Don't undervalue your attributes," he assured her.

Susan accepted his arm as she climbed out of the carriage. She looked every inch the fine lady, wearing a rich blue travelling dress, with bonnet and gloves in cream. All of her clothes were exquisite, despite her stepmother's attempts to make them more risqué. The want of a wedding trousseau hadn't been a disadvantage when deciding what she needed for her first visit to her new home; she had clothes which were beautifully made and suitable for her new position.

Viewing the house in which her husband had been born and brought up in was bound to be of interest to Susan, so it was with weary limbs that she collapsed into bed that night. They'd spent a pleasant day together, but as usual, Miles had kissed Susan on the cheek and wished her a goodnight as he'd left her to enter his own bedchamber.

Restless, Susan tossed and turned for a while. With a racing mind, she climbed out of bed. She might be physically weary, but her brain was not in tune with the rest of her body.

She walked into the large, airy sitting room that separated her chamber from husband's and sat on a plush chair in front of the still-glowing fire. Pulling her shawl closer around her shoulders, she gazed into the low flames.

It had seemed the answer to all of her dreams to be wed to Miles. Instead, it was turning out to be some sort of slow torture. Her hands itched to touch him, but apart from offering his arm and the chaste kiss goodnight, there was no physical contact between them at all.

Sighing, she glanced disinterestedly around the room. Things could be far worse; she should be grateful for what she had. She *was* thankful, but was it so wrong to wish for more? To long for more?

Hearing a noise, Susan stiffened. Miles had never seen her in her nightwear, and the sound was coming from his chamber. If he entered their shared sitting room, would he think she should be more prudently dressed?

The noise came again. She realised it was a sound of anguish. Susan stood and rushed to her husband's chamber door.

Opening the door slowly, Susan peeped in to see an almost identical room to her own, but decorated in reds and golds, compared to the more feminine lemons of her chamber. Miles was in bed, but he was thrashing about and moaning in his sleep. The moans came amidst cries of what seemed like the names of people.

117

Susan assumed it was some sort of nightmare. She paused as Miles's valet entered through the door to the dressing room.

"M'lady," the valet said in a whisper. "I'll see to his lordship. Nothing to worry about."

"He has these nightmares often?" Susan blushed at the unspoken admission that she'd never shared a bed with her husband, but she was not naïve enough to think the valet wouldn't know exactly where his master slept.

"Yes, m'lady. Usually when he's overtired," the valet replied.

"Do we wake him?" Susan asked.

"In a way – it's a case of bringing him out of such a deep sleep, but very slowly. To do so quickly risks his lordship lashing out, not on purpose, of course."

"I understand." Susan nodded. "Please let me attend to him."

"I've done it more times than I care to remember and know exactly what to do," the valet said. His words were gentle, not said to make Susan feel undervalued.

"My husband cared for me in a way I can never truly repay. I'd like to look after him, now that he needs it. I promise to be gentle and careful." Her words were heartfelt. Seeing him distressed made her heart ache for him.

The valet nodded, understanding in his eyes. "Just wake him slowly, my lady. I'd hate for him to hit out and hurt you, imagining he's still on the battlefield."

"If he does it shall be my fault, not his," Susan replied. "Thank you for the advice. Now, get some sleep. I'll call you if I need help."

Once the servant had left, Susan turned toward her husband. She had no idea what to do to ease his pain.

Everything she did would be trial and error, but Miles needed comfort, and she was determined to help him.

She left her shawl at the bottom of the bed and sat next to Miles. Noticing that his bedside table was empty, she realised that he and his valet prepared for this type of situation. If there was nothing on the bedside table, he couldn't harm himself, or inadvertently cause a fire through knocking off a lit candle.

Touching Miles gently, she spoke his name in a whisper. He stilled when she spoke, but after a moment or two his ramblings continued.

Increasing the pressure didn't work, leaving Susan staring down at her husband, trying to decide the next course of action. Soon, making a decision, which although made her blush, was the right thing to do, he walked around to the opposite side of the bed. She climbed in and slowly moved towards Miles, speaking to him the whole time. She had never been so close to him, but all selfish thoughts were cast aside as her priority was Miles's care.

"Miles, it is I, Susan. You're having a bad dream. It's time to wake up. You're safe. Do you hear me, Miles? You're safe and with Susan." Little by little, she moved closer to him under the covers.

It was a strange position to be in, but she maintained her focus. Lying next to him, she started to stroke his face, still speaking to him. "I think we need to plan our exploration of your grounds tomorrow, don't you? Can we go in a gig? I'm sure you must have one. I have to admit, this blasted arm of mine still hurts a little, and riding would aggravate it. You must think I'm a feeble chit, but I shall have to agree with you in that regard. Can you hear me, Miles?"

With a sudden movement, Susan was flung onto her back, her arms roughly yanked above her head. Miles's eyes weren't even open, but his mutterings were urgent and incoherent.

Susan stifled a scream of surprise that would have turned into a yelp of pain had she not been biting her lip. Her arm being treated so roughly brought tears to her eyes, but she would not release a sound of discomfort.

"Miles! Miles! Wake up. It's Susan! You're hurting my arm. Miles! Oh, please wake up!" she sobbed quietly when the pain became too much. The valet's warning suddenly held more meaning than it had when it had been first issued.

Miles paused and then dropped to her side. If her arms hadn't been above her head, he would have landed on them, he was so close. Susan slowly moved her arms onto her chest, still biting her lips as her damaged arm protested at the movement.

He seemed to have fallen into mutterings rather than moans and rantings. Susan forced herself to use her good arm, and although she had to stretch across her body, she stroked Miles's face.

"You're safe, Miles. Everyone is safe. It's Susan. Your wife. I'm here to help," she whispered over and over again.

Eventually, Miles blinked, his eyes unfocused. "Susan?"

"Yes. I'm here. You've been having some dreams. I didn't want you to be alone."

Miles stilled, but then his eyes closed. "Susan," he said quietly, pulling her towards him. Susan turned as he moved her, and he curled around her body.

Wondering what he was going to do once his body was touching the full length of her, Susan stiffened a little.

Miles wrapped his hand around her middle, and his head snuggled into her hair, his breath tickling her neck.

Within a few moments she realised he had fallen asleep, his breathing slow and regular. Relaxing slightly, Susan wrapped her own hand around the one that circled her waist. Feeling a small sense of achievement and pleasure at being able to help him, she eventually let Miles's steady breathing lull her to sleep.

*

Miles awoke knowing he'd had one of his nightmare attacks during the night. He always awoke with a severe headache, although when he blinked awake, he had to admit that the current pounding in his head was less crippling than usual.

Without waiting for instructions, his valet handed him a drink, which Miles sat up to take.

"Was I not as bad as usual last night?" he asked. There was no point in pretending that nothing had happened; they'd both been through the routine enough times for it to be considered almost normal.

"I'm afraid I couldn't say, my lord."

"You didn't hear me? How did you know I needed my drink, then?" Miles handed the empty glass back.

"Lady Longdon said she wished to take care of you. I explained that it was a well-practised routine for us both, but she insisted she would like to remain with you," the former batman and valet admitted.

Miles was horrified. "Susan? My wife saw me like that?"

"She seemed very capable and unperturbed," the valet said reassuringly.

"Good grief, Ashurst, why did you allow her? She's probably halfway back to London by now."

Ashurst coughed lightly. "I do beg pardon, for speaking out of turn, m'lord, but Lady Longdon only left the bed when I entered your chamber. I did offer my sincerest apologies at disturbing her, but she was extremely magnanimous about it and returned to her own room."

Miles flushed. "She stayed the night? In my bed?"

"Yes." It was a conversation neither of them wished to be partaking of, but Miles was not fool enough to pretend his valet, at least, didn't know what the actual state of his marriage was.

Getting out of bed, Miles moved over to the screen to be washed and dressed. He grimaced to himself as the realisation of Susan knowing how damaged he was sank in. She had every right to have him admitted to an asylum, but somehow he knew without seeing her that she wouldn't condemn him. In fact, if he thought through the haze that always followed a disturbed night, he could vaguely remember the feel of her.

He'd never slept with anyone throughout a whole night, not even the mistresses he'd dallied with before he went to the Continent. Once he'd returned and realised what happened during his nightmares, there was no chance he would risk someone seeing him in such a vulnerable state. Feeling a tug of remorse at not being able to properly remember being with Susan all night, he took comfort in the fact that at least unconsciously he'd known she was there, proved by the reduced headache.

An interesting consequence of her presence, he mused.

Chapter 13

When he walked into the dining room, Susan was already seated. She looked up, her expression flushed and a little wary, but Miles smiled at her.

"Good morning," he said, approaching her. "I believe I have you to thank for reduced pain this morning." Bending to place a kiss amongst her curls, he squeezed her shoulder gently.

"I don't understand."

"Whatever happens up here," Miles said, tapping his head, "to cause the nightmares leaves me with a devilishly bad headache. This morning's is not so bad."

"I'm glad." Susan was inadvertently pleased at Miles's response. It made up for her own pain from having her wound so roughly treated. "How often do you suffer from them?"

"Too regularly for my liking," Miles admitted. "You might wish to lock me away when you've heard my shouting out too many times." His words were said flippantly, but there was a hint of worry behind them.

"I'd be a very poor wife if I even considered that for a moment!" Susan responded hotly. "I haven't seen what you have, so why would I condemn you for your nightmares? I'm impressed you can function at all. I'm not sure I could. I screamed when I saw the dead body of Mr. Malone; I'd never have coped with a battlefield full of corpses."

Miles smiled tenderly at Susan. "You are a love. Thank you. Your words mean a lot. Since I returned from France, I normally hate being forced to sleep near anyone who isn't in my inner circle. It's not a weakness I like to acknowledge publicly."

"Your wariness probably makes your situation worse, as you can't properly relax if you are worried about calling out in the night. I promise I won't speak to anyone about it, and I shall do all that I can to help," Susan said.

"I seem to have married myself a treasure." Miles grinned, his usual joviality returning. "As a treat, I think we should explore our land on horseback today."

Susan frowned slightly. "Could we use a vehicle? My arm is still a little sore."

"Is it? Do you need to see a doctor?"

"No! Not at all," Susan answered quickly. "A few days more and I'm sure I'll be back to my old self. I'd prefer to ride my own horses anyway, and they're still in London."

"You're the same as Edith, preferring your own horse flesh to any other," Miles said, amused.

"As a cavalry officer, you should understand our feelings," Susan said.

"I do. Completely. Gig it is, then," Miles said, tucking into his plateful of food.

Susan watched him surreptitiously. He was everything she'd hoped he would be as a husband, except for being in love with her, of course. She ached to touch him. Cursing herself for her feelings of pleasure at being next to him for most of the night, she took a sip of her tea. It had been exquisite lying in the same bed as him, with his body wrapped around hers. Wanton she might be, but she ached for the physicality a loving marriage brought, even if there was only love on one side.

124

Miles was perfect. She just wished he wanted her as a wife in the truest sense of the word. For now, she would have to be content with his liking her, but her heart longed for the ability turn liking into loving.

*

Visiting tenants and exploring the land filled Susan with the excitement of being mistress of her own home. She chattered as they returned to the house after many hours of exploration.

"I'm not surprised that everything appears in order on your estate. You don't come across as a neglectful landlord," Susan said as they travelled along in their gig.

"Thank you, but my father and elder brother should have the credit, not me," Miles said. "I've been away for so many years, anything could have happened to the estate if I'd been in charge. It was strange coming home and knowing I was head of the family." He acknowledged some of the reality of the changes in his family.

"You and Edith suffered too much loss in a short time."

"Yes. To go from having a mother, father, two brothers and a sister to a mother and sister was a sobering experience," he said. "I'm not sure if I really grieved properly for them. I'm ashamed to admit that I don't know if Edith did either. She was wrapped up in supporting Mother and keeping the estate functioning until I returned. She coped admirably, when she was actually very young to take on such a burden."

"I miss her, and she's not been gone very long," Susan said.

"Tiring of me already?" Miles asked.

"Oh, definitely." Susan laughed. "I'm hoping we'll spend quite a bit of time with them when they return from their marriage trip."

"It depends on if you like to spend time in the country," Miles said. "I know Edith has had enough of London, and Ralph never was very keen. They're a perfect match in that regard, at least."

Shooting Miles a sideways look, feeling bold, Susan squeezed his hand. "They are a good match in every regard. You worry too much."

Miles patted her hand and smiled. "I know. She's just even more precious to me than ever now. She'd ridicule me if she realised, although I think she suspects."

"I don't know what she will make of our pairing." Susan turned away to look at the house they were approaching.

"You've told her the full story. She will understand," Miles assured her.

"Yes, you're right. She'll understand everything," Susan said, recalling the conversation she'd had with her friend about the affection she felt for Edith's brother.

*

Eight days later, Susan was seated in the drawing room at her new home in London when the door burst open and Edith rushed in.

"Susan! Oh my goodness me! I am so glad you're here alone! Where's Mother? That doesn't matter – I'm happy to get the opportunity to speak to you without being in her presence. Tell me all that has happened. Your letter was such a surprise!" Edith babbled. She was dressed for the outdoors and looked slightly windswept, but Susan noticed

126

another change in her friend. Happiness radiated from her. Always one to be forceful, Edith had been the queen of the sharp retort and arch look. Her expression now was warm and happy. Marriage clearly suited her.

Laughing, Susan stood to greet her friend and now sister-in-law. "Edith! What are you doing here? You are supposed to be on your wedding trip!"

"I told Ralph we had to return immediately. I might have missed your wedding, but I needed to see you both. I think Ralph was as curious as I was because he offered no complaint," Edith said.

She was very like her brother, with dark brown hair and clear grey eyes. Edith was always prone to speak her mind and had reprimanded the beaux of society whenever she'd thought they were being ridiculous in trying to court her, especially the ones who had made it plain it was her fortune they were interested in. This had resulted in many men giving her a wide berth, particularly when they'd seen the glint in her mother's eyes when alighting on potential suitors. It hadn't made for a happy season for Edith.

"Oh dear," Susan groaned. "You must despise me."

"Why ever would I do that?" Edith asked. "You are my best friend, and now you are my sister. What more could I want?"

"But you know of my true feelings," Susan whispered. "I promise I contrived none of the events to ensnare your brother."

"Of course you didn't!" Edith said. Taking Susan's hands in hers, she led her to a sofa on which they could sit side by side. "Now, come, tell me it all from the beginning."

*

127

"I thought you were about as likely to marry as I was," Ralph said, blowing out a cloud of smoke from the cigar his friend had lit for him.

"As you are wed, that's not the best of comparisons," Miles responded dryly.

"Perhaps not. But rescuing Miss King – sorry, Lady Longdon – I can understand. Becoming leg-shackled seems a little excessive – unless you wanted to, of course. In that case I would sincerely congratulate you," Ralph said. He was a man not prone to smiling much, and his dark, angular features made him look more severe than he was. Since his marriage, he was beginning to slowly turn into a man more relaxed and more able to enter into his wife's funning, but it was going to be a long time before a major change took place.

"No. I didn't want to," Miles admitted. "A bloody bet in White's meant that I had little choice, or she would be ruined. Her damned stepmother had spread it around town that she'd eloped as some sort of romantic flight. The bloody idiot. She's done Susan no favours since she's been married to King. Added to which, he's not got the backbone to stand up to his wife, I don't think."

"It's not an unusual story."

"No. But I think it's affected Susan's feelings of self-worth. Which weren't helped when my own mother behaved disgracefully when we returned home," Miles said with a grimace.

"Looks like you've had a right time of it."

"It's not been too bad since we made our vows," Miles said. "She's a pleasant girl."

"Is that the best you can utter?" Ralph mocked.

Flushing, Miles defended his words. "It can never be passed off as a love match to anyone who truly knows us, although that's what we're saying to anyone else. A long-standing secret affection and regard."

"Which will be shown to be incorrect the moment people see you, if you consider your wife as merely 'pleasant'."

Miles shrugged. "It's been a few days. I'm sure we'll settle into what is now our lot in life."

"Does the poor chit realise she's married a damned cold fish?" Ralph scoffed.

A memory of Susan's body against his flashed through Miles's mind.

Ralph saw his friend's expression change. "Ah, I think there is hope for you after all."

"You talk rubbish," Miles replied.

"I hope not, or both of you will suffer as a result."

*

"And isn't married life wonderful?" Edith asked after Susan had told her everything that had happened over the last few weeks.

"I don't think we have quite settled into being comfortable with each other just yet." Susan looked at Edith, a blush on her cheeks.

"You aren't living as man and wife?" Edith exclaimed.

"Oh, please, Edith!" Susan appealed to her friend. "Of course we aren't. It was a marriage of convenience, to stop my ruination. I can't expect anything else."

"But you love Miles," Edith pointed out.

"You know that and I know it, but he doesn't," Susan hissed.

"It's about time he did, then."

"No! What if he rejected me, Edith? I couldn't face him. I already feel a complete imposter, but we are friends. I can't risk having him turn away from me if he were to find out I've been in love with him for years."

"Oh, my dear Susan! He would be a fool to reject sincere affection." Edith pulled Susan into an embrace.

"Oh, don't be nice to me, Edith," Susan said, pulling away a little. "I think I will cry if you do. I have to accept my position and be grateful for what I have. As your brother said, we rub along quite well. That has to be enough."

"I never thought I'd say that Miles is chuckle-headed, but he is," Edith said quietly. "I'm sorry a marriage to him is a disaster. You deserve more than that."

"It's not his fault. It isn't anyone's apart from that scoundrel, Sage."

"Yes, I certainly put all the blame on him, but I am saddened that you are in a loveless marriage. It's ironic that it's with the man you love. In fact, I think it's cruel that you should be so," Edith said gently grasping Susan's hands in an act of comfort.

"No. I am happy to spend time with him and to try to be as good a wife as I can in the circumstances," Susan said, for the first time lying to her closest friend.

*

"My brother is a total blockhead!" Edith exclaimed once she was seated in her own carriage, snuggled up to her husband.

"I can't disagree with you on that score," Ralph answered, snaking his arms around his wife and kissing her.

"Stop!" Edith laughed. "I'm trying to curse my brother to the devil."

"I'd much rather kiss you to distraction."

"You do that all the time."

"Good. Now let me do it some more."

"No!" Edith said, using her hands to push against Ralph's chest. She didn't push herself far away; she didn't like being away from him for very long.

Ralph sighed. "Speak to me quickly, and then at least I can kiss you some of the way home. I told the coachman to take the long route. I've decided we live too close to your brother. How can I kiss you senseless in ten minutes?"

"You're incorrigible." Edith smiled, before becoming serious. "Susan has been in love with Miles for an age."

"That will help their story stand up to scrutiny."

"Not when they are both acting like mere acquaintances and not a newly married couple," Edith scoffed.

"I pointed out something similar to Miles," Ralph said. "But marriages aren't always a love match."

"I agree, but theirs is supposed to be," Edith said. "They've married to stop Susan being ruined, but surely the cads who placed bets will be watching them closely? It just seems a scheme doomed to failure when it should be guaranteed a success. They deserve happiness for different reasons, but I'm sure if they were more open towards each other, the rest would follow naturally."

"I admit, I thought it a slightly odd bet," Ralph said. "But I'm sure they'll be fine."

"You are more confident than I," Edith admitted. "And I feel so sorry for Susan. I keep trying to think if there is anything we can do to help."

"No. No. No," Ralph said firmly. "If we intervened it would end in disaster."

"But if we were successful …"

"I don't expect you to be subservient in many situations," Ralph said. "But in this case, you must trust me. Don't interfere."

Edith pouted, but then frowned. "I do think the bet was done in very poor taste."

"Yet another reason to dislike the society we belong to," Ralph said.

"I'm glad we'll be spending our time in the country."

"Will we leave soon?" Ralph asked hopefully.

"Could we stay just a little while to show support for Miles and Susan?"

"Edith—" Ralph warned.

"I promise I won't meddle," his dutiful wife said. "Supporting them isn't the same as getting involved in their situation."

"As long as it isn't interfering by another name."

"Of course not, my love. Now, what was it you were saying about kissing?"

Chapter 14

Susan watched as her maid dressed her hair with extra care. Tonight was the gathering of some of their friends to celebrate her nuptials. She wished she could cancel the whole thing, but her father insisted on showing off her achievement of securing a titled, wealthy man. At least she'd convinced him not to have a grand ball. That she couldn't have borne.

Closing her eyes for a moment, she swallowed. The last few days had been difficult to say the least. Being out in society, their situation seen as the *on dit* of the season, hadn't been what she'd intended. Wherever they went as a couple, they were watched, fussed over and asked questions about their escapade. She'd found the whole thing trying enough, but what was worse was the increased tightness of Miles's smiles and the way he seemed to be distancing himself from her.

Any hope of developing the friendship they'd shared at the start seemed impossible when it felt they were the most popular couple in the whole of London. Which meant that as soon as they entered a room, they were separated, the gentlemen congratulating Miles and calling him a sly dog and the women crowding around Susan, needing to hear every romantic detail. She'd never been so popular in the whole of her four seasons, and she hated it.

She was surprised that she hadn't woken in the night screaming at the pressure she felt under. She tried to breathe slowly to gain control of her inner turmoil.

Hopefully, after this evening they could start to withdraw a little from scrutiny and find time to relax.

Walking down the stairs, she smiled to see Edith and Ralph waiting for her at the bottom of the staircase. She looked at Miles with a smile, which he returned, but her own faltered when she saw once more it no longer reached his eyes.

Her mother-in-law had feigned illness to avoid being with her daughter. A rift had developed between the pair prior to Edith marrying, and each woman seemed as stubborn as the other when it came to overcoming their argument. In some respects Susan had been relieved; she knew Miles's mother hadn't believed their story, so there was less chance their charade would be discovered if her mother-in-law was avoiding entertainments. It was better that the dowager's two house guests fuss over her; they would make her feel better than she would have if attending the meal.

"You look delightful," Edith said. "That colour really suits you, doesn't it, Miles?"

Susan was wearing a mint-green silk gown with cream edging. She had paired it with emeralds, around her neck and in her hair. On her wedding, she'd inherited her mother's jewels, and Susan had chosen to wear some of her mother's favourite pieces as a homage to her.

"You look lovely," Miles said, stepping forward to offer her his arm. "Come, let's get this over with."

His words silenced the others, and they left the house. Edith exchanged a look of concern with her husband, but he just shook his head in warning.

The couples walked the short distance to the Kind household rather than take a carriage. A blaze of lights greeted them as they entered the open doorway. They were the first to arrive, as the honoured guests, but had been late enough for Mr. King to come out into the hallway the moment they arrived.

"At last!" Mr. King said, almost throwing his hands in the air. "Where have you been?"

"It was my fault, Papa. I took too long in dressing." Susan approached her father and kissed him on the cheek. "No one has arrived yet, surely?"

"No. But I was preparing to ask that any arriving coaches be sent around the streets for another few minutes."

Susan laughed. "We have invited our closest friends. They wouldn't have minded getting here before us."

"Yes. Yes. Come. Come. Let's go into the drawing room." Mr. King hurried them into the large room as soon as shawls and greatcoats had been dispensed with.

After greeting Mrs. King, they were handed drinks, which had barely touched their lips before Jones and Dunn were shown in, followed closely by the other thirty invitees.

The two captains made a fuss of Susan and soon had her laughing, along with Edith, which gave Ralph the opportunity to approach Miles.

"I suggest you look less as if you're being led to the gallows and more that you are pleased with your new wife, or those nearest and dearest to you will start to doubt your sincerity as a new husband," Ralph cautioned quietly.

"There is nothing wrong with my wife," Miles said. "It's this bloody farce of a situation we're in that I dislike."

"Edith is already worrying and trying to plot ways of making you fall in love." A half-smile formed on Ralph's lips when he saw the horror on Miles's face as his words sank in.

"Do. Not. Let. Her. Interfere," Miles said through gritted teeth.

"I've warned her, but you know what effect that will have on her, don't you?"

"What?"

"Absolutely none." Ralph shrugged. "Your sister has a mind of her own. And it's a strong one."

"I bloody know it," Miles said. "If she starts trying to fix things, I'll kick you both to your pile in the country."

"Leave me out of it," Ralph said with a laugh, before sobering slightly. "You do need to decide what you are going to do if you can't keep up the charade. Perhaps you need another trip to the country yourself to take the pressure off you both."

Miles sighed. "I think I do need an escape."

"An escape? From what?" Dunn drawled from behind Miles. "Not that pretty wife of yours, surely?"

"No. Not her," Miles said, but his two friends frowned at the unenthusiastic way the words were delivered.

"Married life not what you hoped?" Dunn asked, trying to appear jovial but watching Miles closely.

"Let's be honest, it was doomed from the start, wasn't it?"

"Enough of this!" Ralph hissed. "Put a damned smile on your face and join your guests. If you upset your wife, *mine* will be distraught, and I won't have her so. Do you hear me?"

"Loud and clear." Miles walked away from the pair, a fixed smile on his face.

Dunn was quiet for a few moments before speaking. "I didn't think it would come to this. I've never seen him so serious."

"Did you not?" Ralph asked. "Two people forced together purely because of circumstance. One with few

136

options, and the other sacrificing himself to do the right thing. How could that have possibly gone well?"

Looking abashed, Dunn coughed a little. "You didn't see what we did on the boat. She's besotted with him, and he likes her, probably just as much, but doesn't realise it."

"And you thought you could force them together and all would be well," Ralph said, looking candidly at the other man. "I thought the bet was an odd circumstance as soon as I heard about it."

"For God's sake, don't mention it to Miles! He believes it's genuine," Dunn said hurriedly. "If he found out ..."

"I'm not a fool," Ralph responded with derision.

"Good. We'll just have to make tonight a good one. Miles is a sociable creature; he'll relax as the night goes on."

"I'd start by making sure his glass is never empty," Ralph advised before walking off.

*

Mrs. King indicated that her daughter should be the one handing out the teas, along with Edith. When the task was finished, Edith had been delayed by an acquaintance, who encouraged her to sit and tell them all about her own wedding, which she did willingly.

Susan returned to her stepmother. "Is there anything else I can do to help?"

"No. I think you can consider the night a success," Mrs. King replied.

"Thank you for keeping the event small. I know Papa would have preferred a large gathering."

"I wouldn't have him wasting further money on you. You have had enough indulgence from us. We can wash our hands of you now you've found someone to take you on." Mrs. King's smile never wavered, nor did her tone reveal the dislike behind the words.

"I am more than happy with my husband," Susan said primly. "I wish you could be happy for me."

"I'm sure you are. He's one of the catches, if not *the* catch, of the season," Mrs. King sneered. "What I'd like to know is how the devil you managed to persuade him to marry you. I'm sure it will come out at some point. These things tend to do."

"Please excuse me. I think Mrs. Whitworth needs a refill," Susan said, refusing to be drawn further. She wasn't confident she could lie convincingly enough in response to her stepmother's suspicions, and she couldn't risk her gaining the slightest inkling about the bet. If that happened, it would be known throughout society; Susan was sure of it. A slight headache developed behind her eyes with the strain of maintaining her happy façade.

After the gentlemen joined the ladies in the drawing room, there were calls for dancing. The carpets were moved back, and a volunteer seated herself at the piano. Miles led Susan out to the top of the first set as the leading couple.

"Have you had an enjoyable evening?" he asked as they passed each other in the dance.

"You haven't," Susan replied.

Looking a little stunned at his wife's response, Miles frowned. "What makes you say that?"

"I have known you for years, admittedly with an absence whilst you were at war, but I know you well enough to realise when you are putting on a show for the guests and yet wish yourself miles from here," Susan said, emboldened by the movement of the dance. She could speak her mind without necessarily needing to look into Miles's eyes whilst she did it.

"Do you not?" Miles asked.

"In some respects, yes, probably as much as you, but perhaps for different reasons."

"Oh?"

"You are regretting your decision to help. I'd just rather be away from prying eyes. I've never sought to be the centre of attention, and this situation has us both firmly set as the centre of society," Susan said.

"It was the right thing to do," Miles responded, not denying her assessment.

"One that has condemned you to a life you didn't wish to have." The lump in the pit of Susan's stomach was ever increasing in size.

"That neither of us wished to have."

"Perhaps not," Susan said, in the closest thing to a declaration of her feelings that she would ever make. "When we return to Barrowfoot House we shall make plans as to how we can resolve this in some way."

"I don't understand how anything can change," Miles said. "We've made the choice about what was best."

"No. You were forced into a decision, and you're not happy. I'm not going to stand by and watch you suffer," Susan said firmly, but quietly enough that she wasn't overheard by the other dancers. Anyone looking at them would presume they were having a whispered conversation of the newly wed.

"You make it sound as if I hate being with you," Miles said. "I don't. I do want you to believe that."

"Maybe not at the moment, but you will eventually." Susan seemed to sag as she spoke the words. "I need to do something before that happens."

Miles looked at his wife in concern. Her words worried him more than he would have anticipated. He did hate the situation. He detested it with a passion, but he was being honest when he'd admitted his ire wasn't aimed at her. He already knew she was loving and considerate of others. She was a genuinely decent person.

"I promise one way or another you will be free to carry out your life as you would wish. Perhaps not to marry the person you would have chosen, but in all other aspects, you will have a happier life than you would with me," Susan said seriously.

"Susan, I—" Miles started, desperate to turn the conversation from the direction in which it was heading.

The music stopped, and they honoured each other. Susan took the opportunity to immediately separate herself from her husband. It felt as if her heart was breaking, but her smile never wavered. She would not allow any chance of further gossip attaching itself to Miles. He'd sacrificed enough for her. It was time to leave him. And soon.

Chapter 15

It was inevitable that Susan wouldn't be able to sleep. She crept into her shared sitting room long after everyone else had retired. She'd had the forethought to ask the maid to ensure there was coal on the fire to keep the room warm.

Now, sitting in front of the blazing fire, she listlessly looked into the flames. She would take herself to the outer reaches of Scotland and leave Miles to enjoy society as much or as little as he wished. It wouldn't be long before people accepted that she'd been a little strange from the beginning and congratulated him on a fortunate escape. Then he could have what mistresses he wished and forget about her completely.

Tears trickled down her face as she resolved to release her husband. The man she loved more than any other person she had ever known, and yet even now she couldn't have him. Bound together in the eyes of God and the law, and yet it was worse than if they'd never been joined. He was hers in name only and would never be anything else.

A sob escaped her lips. She quickly covered her mouth, fearing she'd be heard in Miles's room. On hearing a noise, she thought she had been overheard, but then she realised it was Miles, once more having a nightmare.

Wiping her eyes, she stood and walked quickly to the door leading to his chamber. She opened it quietly and peeped in to see her husband thrashing about in his bed.

With no other thought than to soothe his terrors, she immediately went to him and started to speak quietly and reassuringly. She was prepared for if he should grab for her as he had last time.

When Ashurst, the valet, entered the room, he showed no surprise at seeing Susan already there.

"After this evening, it's no real surprise he's disturbed," Susan said.

"He seemed a little agitated when being undressed, m'lady," Ashurst admitted.

"I'll stay with him," Susan said, not looking at the valet, to prevent him seeing her new tears at his words.

"You must be exhausted, m'lady, after your evening's entertainment. I'm quite happy to remain with his lordship."

"No. I wouldn't sleep knowing he was suffering. You get off to bed. I promise I will call you if I need you."

"I won't venture in early tomorrow," Ashurst said. "But if you'll allow me to make up his lordship's drink now, you can give it to him as soon as he awakens. It helps with the headache that follows a disturbed night."

Susan blushed slightly. "Thank you."

She waited until the valet had prepared the vital drink, and then, with a bow and a smile of encouragement, he left her alone.

Susan climbed into the bed. Talking all the time, she stroked Miles's face as he mumbled, but he seemed to settle quicker than he had the first time she'd experienced his nightmares. She continued to speak gently to him and touch him tenderly; over and over she reassured him that he was safe with her and there was no need to worry. Eventually, he calmed, and she lay down on the pillow next to him and watched him sleep.

It was with mixed pleasure she observed him, but she wouldn't have returned to her own chamber for anything. Being able to look on his face and see him when he was at peace at last was too much of a temptation for her. He looked younger, but the frown lines around his eyes and across his forehead had indented permanent grooves that no amount of laughing or an easier life would erase.

The urge to touch him was irresistible. Susan used her fingers to trace the outline of the frown lines, before following the curve of his face. His lips parted slightly at her touch, and she paused, afraid she'd disturbed him or caused his nightmares to return.

Sighing, Miles settled back into a regular breathing rhythm, and Susan relaxed once more. She rested her head on the pillow and fell asleep, watching the man she adored.

On waking, Susan stilled. She was facing away from the direction in which she'd fallen asleep. She was wrapped in an embrace, with Miles. His arms curled around her middle, holding her against his body. It was the second time she'd shared such a closeness with him – with anyone – and it felt wonderful. Afraid to move, yet more in fear of him waking and pulling away from her in disgust, she started to slowly wriggle away.

"And where do you think you're going?" said the low, gravelly voice of her husband.

Susan was thankful her cheeks couldn't be seen, because they burned with embarrassment. "I didn't wish to disturb you."

Miles pulled her tight against him, burying his face in her hair.

Susan tried not to stiffen in response at the intimate movement. Her heart was pounding with nerves and pleasure.

"You aren't disturbing me. In fact, this is a lovely way to wake up," Miles said, kissing her hair.

Susan shivered at his touch, but tried to focus on his care. Not easy when it seemed all her dreams had suddenly become a reality. "Ashurst has prepared your drink. Let me get it for you."

"It was a bad night, was it?" Miles asked.

"Yes. Although it didn't seem as bad as the first time I saw you disturbed," Susan said. She would have laughed at the extraordinary situation if she hadn't been pulsing with emotions at her position. Thoughts were tumbling through her mind. Was it an after-effect of his nightmare? Or was he teasing her? No. He wouldn't be that cruel. Her mind was in turmoil, but her body was responding to his actions.

"It seems you have a good effect on me when I'm troubled. My headache isn't too severe," Miles said.

"You still should have the drink."

"But that would mean you climbing out of this bed, and I don't want you to."

"Oh."

Miles tugged Susan gently onto her back so he could look into her eyes. He'd woken up wondering where the devil he was and whom he was with, and slowly he'd realised. Instead of being horrified and wishing to extract himself from the delicate situation, he'd relished the feel of his wife in his arms. Her curves fitted against him, which made him respond in a way he hadn't expected. "You look wonderfully dishevelled, Lady Longdon." He smiled when Susan blushed a deeper red. "I will not keep you here against your will, but I'd like you to stay."

"I-I'd like to stay."

Smiling again, Miles kissed her nose. "Good. Now am I allowed to kiss you as a wife should be kissed, or do you wish to remain in my arms and we can just talk?" Miles asked. He was fully aware that the previous evening she'd had thoughts of leaving him. The realisation had worried and upset him more than he would have ever imagined. Now, she was here, in his arms, and he wanted to make her his wife in every sense of the word. He'd never felt possessive about anything or anyone before, but he did with Susan the moment he realised she was considering leaving him. It had been part of the reason he'd gone to bed so agitated, worrying about how he would feel without Susan in his life. That he didn't recognise it as affection was down to fear of considering his true feelings; instead he'd excused it to himself as worry about how she would suffer being removed from friends and family.

"Do as you would wish," Susan replied, watching Miles carefully.

"But what if it isn't what you want me to do?"

"It will be," Susan admitted.

"Good. Because I really want to kiss you thoroughly, Susan," Miles said, watching her mouth open in a silent 'o'. "And I think you want me to kiss you too."

Neither uttered another word as Miles proved to Susan that sometimes what you wish for can be as good as, if not better than, you'd imagined.

*

Miles awoke at the sound of rustling in his room. Susan was still wrapped in his embrace. Not wishing to disturb her, he slowly lifted his head to see his valet moving slowly into the room.

The valet paused when he noticed Miles's gaze on him. "M'lord?" he whispered.

145

"Breakfast in our sitting room, and no further disturbances for either of us," Miles whispered in return. Receiving a nod of understanding from the retreating valet, he snuggled back into his wife.

"I will never be able to face Ashurst again after his seeing me in such a way," Susan said quietly as the door clicked shut.

"I shall have to dismiss him, then, because I like waking up like this."

Susan's heart soared at the words, and she couldn't prevent a laugh escaping. "We would send all the servants into shock if we slept in the same bed every night."

Moving so he could look into her eyes, Miles kissed her gently. "I've never slept with anyone all night before. I never thought I could."

"Because of your nightmares?"

"Yes. The first time I was told you'd heard them, I half expected to be carted off to the asylum in the morning," he said.

"Why would I do that when it is what you've seen defending every one of us that has caused them in the first place? I'd be a very poor woman to repay you in such a way."

"It would be the perfect excuse to rid yourself of an unwanted husband."

Susan looked away, her expression pained.

"What is it? Tell me," Miles said softly.

"You aren't unwanted," Susan admitted shyly. "I shall be forever sorry on your account that you were forced into this situation, but I have nothing to be remorseful of."

"You really are a sweet girl." Miles gave her another gentle kiss. "You always say the right things. I wish I had that ability. I'm more like a bumbling idiot."

"Not to me you aren't."

"I like an adoring wife. I could get used to it." Miles smiled down at Susan. A gentle knock on the door to the sitting room caught his attention. "Now, come, my dear. I think breakfast has been served next door."

"I must dress," Susan said, starting to move.

"Must you?"

"W-well, there will be people calling soon, and your mother …"

"We aren't at home to callers, and my mother is more than capable of entertaining herself. She has two friends residing with her, who pander to her every whim," Miles said firmly. "We haven't had two moments together. I think it's about time we did."

When Miles had wrapped himself in his own banyan, he pulled a second out of his wardrobe. Wrapping it around Susan and tying it at the waist, he smiled. "It is far too long and could almost go around you twice, but I like the thought of my wife in my clothing. Come, let us eat before I faint from lack of sustenance."

Entering the sitting room, Susan blinked at the amount of food on the table. Meats, bread, cheeses, pie, eggs, bacon and chicken filled the space.

"Excellent." Miles crossed the room in easy strides and sat himself down. "I'm ravenous. Come and tuck in. You must be too."

Smiling, Susan seated herself opposite her husband. Although the sleeves of the banyan very often got in the way, she relished every moment of watching Miles enjoy his food. After a long while of eating, he finally sat back replete.

"I do love a hearty breakfast," he said contentedly.

"I'll be surprised if you eat for the rest of the day," Susan teased.

"Oh, I'll be ready for luncheon, don't you worry."

"Am I to expect a husband with a widening girth as the years go by?" Susan asked archly.

"Would it bother you if you did?"

"No. Not at all," she said with a shy smile.

Miles smiled back. "That's a good answer. Especially as it seems that all your foolish thoughts about leaving me have been put to rest," he said gently.

Susan's eyes glanced at his before looking at her hands, now clasped together. "I still don't think it's fair to force you to remain in a situation that gives you so much discomfort. You didn't enjoy yesterday evening, which was the reason you had a disturbed night. I'm sure the two are linked."

"There is always a link between what happens in the day and my nightmares. It seems when my equilibrium is upset in some way, the result is a bad night. I've tried drinking myself into oblivion when I've had a hard day, but all that it achieves is that the headache is worse in the morning," Miles said.

"It must be hard to bear."

"People have far worse reminders of what we went through. But that's not a concern at the moment. I want you to stop talking about your leaving and my being the martyr in all of this. I don't recall feeling anything but pleasure this morning when we decided to be man and wife in the truest sense. That's hardly the sign of a husband to be pitied, is it?"

Susan blushed. "But you wouldn't have picked me had you married of your own free will."

"No. I wouldn't. But that doesn't mean to say that I'm unhappy with you. For I'm not, Susan. You have to believe that."

148

"You are very kind," Susan responded, but she didn't believe him. How could he be happy with her when there were any number of beautiful women who would have given him what she had and more?

Miles stood, held out his hands and lifted Susan to her feet. "You have to believe one aspect of my personality. I'm not saying that all men are the same, because they aren't, but I can't have relations with someone if I'm not attracted to or fond of them. It's isn't in my nature to take pleasure from just anyone. Do you understand what I'm saying, Susan?"

"I think so."

"I hope I can prove to you that I can be a good husband and we will make a good match of this," Miles assured his wife. The morning had been a revelation for him, and for the first time since they'd returned to London, he wasn't feeling so desolate. He would be forever thankful that Susan had climbed into his bed to comfort him. "Now, come, let's return to my chamber."

"We can't!" Susan exclaimed.

Miles raised an eyebrow. "You'd rather use your chamber?"

"No. I mean ... the servants ..."

"Are paid very well and won't disturb us. We have days of catching up to do," Miles said, lifting Susan into his arms and walking back into his room.

Susan rested her head on his shoulder. He didn't love her, but he'd told her he was fond of her. That would be enough. She could be happy with that, for she loved him so much, it must be enough for them both.

Chapter 16

Susan looked up with a smile and a blush when Edith walked into the drawing room. Edith paused, looking around the room.

"Where's Mama?" she asked in surprise.

"She's gone to a public breakfast," Susan explained. "I don't think she can accustom herself to the fact that I've usurped her as lady of the house, so she tends to organise visits instead of sharing morning calls with me."

Rolling her eyes, Edith sat down. "I thought by coming back to London I'd be forced to see her and we'd have to sort out our differences. It appears not. I haven't actually been in her company since our return." Edith and her mother had argued almost irreparably when she'd refused the marriage proposal from Mr. Sage. None of them were to realise that her refusal would stir him into taking drastic action against Susan to achieve his aim of marrying an heiress.

"I haven't spent much time with her either," Susan said. "It's a shame, but understandable that she wanted a bride of the highest quality for her son."

"Poppycock!" Edith exclaimed. "You are worth a dozen of the bird-witted, simpering specimens who populate the ballrooms."

"Yet I was on the shelf at three and twenty, and most of them are married in their first season," Susan pointed out reasonably.

"That's because most men don't know what's good for them!" Edith responded tartly. "They rue the day they married before too long. Look around you at the next ball you attend and see how many men look dejected and browbeaten. There are lots."

Laughing at her friend, Susan shook her head. "I admit to only enjoying the entertainments when you are there to point out the ridiculous. I've hated being the centre of attention since my return. You know I prefer being on the edges of society."

"Yes. You and Miles both. That is yet another reason why you are a perfect match." Edith narrowed her eyes at her friend. "You're looking well this morning, my dear."

"Am I?" Susan said, blushing under the close scrutiny.

"Oh my goodness! There have been developments!" Edith immediately moved to Susan's side and grabbed her hands. "Has my brother seen your true value?"

"I'm not sure about that, but we have become closer," Susan admitted, her cheeks aflame.

"Isn't true married life wonderful?" Edith asked. "I never imagined how it could be, in all honesty, but it's the most loving, satisfying thing, is it not?"

"It is," Susan said quietly. "I didn't think I could love your brother more, but I've found out my affection for him keeps increasing."

"That is all I would wish to hear. I'm sure he feels the same about you."

"I'm not foolish enough to believe that," Susan responded quickly. "I know he likes me, and that is all I can expect."

"Nonsense! If he isn't halfway to being in love with you, I don't know my brother!" Edith said with conviction.

"Now, I think it's about time we planned a horse ride out. Just the four of us."

Susan's arm was still giving her discomfort, so although she was willing and eager to get back in the saddle, she didn't want the first ride to be a long one. Agreeing to venture only as far as Hyde Park, the four met up the following morning.

Both Susan and Edith were excellent horsewomen, and they led the way into the park, chattering away.

"We're early enough that we should be able to gather some speed through the park," Edith said. "Will you be able to manage a little canter?"

"I should think it would be a good opportunity to try it," Susan said. "If there are no after-effects, I can venture further in a day or two."

"Miles looks relaxed," Edith said with an arch look.

"He, like me, is happier out of doors," Susan said, blushing. She'd spent the night with Miles. It had been passionate for them both, and although Susan would have liked the closeness to continue all day, she wasn't foolish enough to push too far too soon.

"I'm glad to see your eyes sparkling and looking happy. I want nothing other than you both to be content," Edith said. "Now, come let's burn off some of these horses' energy!" With a flick of the reins, Edith moved forward. Susan followed, closely chased by Miles and Ralph.

Not speaking until Susan slowed her own beast down to a gentle trot, Miles approached her.

"Are you in pain?" he asked. "Should we return home?"

"No. It's just a little discomfort," Susan said. "I'm being overcautious during this outing in the hope that I'll be able to go further the next time we venture out."

"As long as you're sure," Miles said.

"Yes."

A crack from the vicinity of the bushes startled the humans and horses alike. Susan's animal reared, and although she remained seated, she struggled to gain control. Once the four hooves were back on the ground, the horse set off at a gallop.

Susan clung to its mane, whilst at the same time trying to slow the animal down without damaging herself or the horse. She heard shouts behind her and was sure the others were in pursuit. Not one for panicking, as she was a competent horsewoman, she slowly but surely slowed the alarmed horse down until she came to a stop. Susan slid off the animal and moved to its front to check it over for any injuries.

Miles, Edith and Ralph all came to a halt seconds after Susan had, and each dismounted. Miles was immediately at his wife's side. Taking hold of her hands, he spun her to face him.

"Are you hurt?" he demanded.

"No. Not at all," Susan replied.

"What about your arm?"

Susan rubbed it. "I honestly don't know. I think the concentration on taking care of Star was enough to focus my mind away from my wound."

"I thought you'd take a tumble before you managed to get the situation under control," Miles said, the feeling of utter terror still pulsing through his veins.

"Are you questioning my horsemanship?" Susan asked indignantly.

"No," Miles said with a slight smile. "Not usually, anyway. But you are at a slight disadvantage at the moment."

"I'm fine. Truly," Susan said, his concern warming her insides.

"Let's walk the horses back," Edith suggested, interrupting the conversation. The incident had shaken them all.

"Very well," Susan replied. There was no point in trying to convince them that she was well enough to ride back. She was a little shaken, although she wouldn't admit it.

Ralph approached Miles, allowing the two women to lead the way. He waited until the ladies were deep in conversation before he spoke. "That was a gunshot."

"Yes. And very close to us," Miles said grimly.

"Who would be firing a gun in the middle of Hyde Park?"

"Did you see anything?"

"No. I admit I should have stayed behind, but my first thought was to make sure Susan didn't require any help, when in reality you could have done that," Ralph said.

"I thought she'd be thrown because of her not being up to snuff," Miles admitted. "I don't think I've ever been as afraid of anything in my life! I just kept thinking that I had to reach her in time."

"She's an experienced horsewoman, injured or not," Ralph said, looking interestedly at his friend. "Shall we try to find where the shot came from?"

"I doubt there's much point. Whatever or whoever it was must have seen the result of their stupidity and have disappeared now," Miles reasoned. "Let's just get Susan home."

*

The next day Ralph joined Miles in White's. He rarely attended the establishment, but he was under strict instructions from his wife to check on her brother and see if he would admit to a growing affection for Susan. Ralph, not usually one to take such trouble over interfering into another's life, had decided that if he didn't give his wife assurances, she would go blundering in herself. As he had concealed the reality of the bet from his wife and brother-in-law, he had a vested interest in ensuring that Miles remained unaware of the contrivance of his other friends.

The two men sat opposite each other, sipping a fine brandy and enjoying the atmosphere of the club.

"Are we to plan a further trip out, now Susan is convinced the ride to Hyde Park didn't leave her with any long-lasting effects?" Ralph asked.

"I suppose that depends on whether you are to remain in London long," Miles said. "Will you not be returning to your mother soon?" Ralph's mother had an illness that could strike her at any time, which had resulted in Ralph remaining very much in the background of society. He hadn't wanted people to know his mother had an affliction, but if he had been in the centre of the season it would have been noticed that he was very often called home.

"Mother is determined to live, not just exist, and part of her decision was to convince me that I had to live my own life. I get regular updates from her and the staff, and although she's taking life very easy, she's being more sociable than she has been up to now," Ralph explained.

"Good for her. I'm still surprised at your remaining in the city. I thought you were going to settle in the country quicker than you clearly intend on doing. I know Edith dislikes London as much as you do."

155

"Edith is worried about you, so she is determined to stay here until she's happy you can cope without her," Ralph admitted. There was no point in lying to Miles in that regard.

Miles snorted. "Because I haven't been able to manage my affairs until now. You have a meddling wife."

"But a gorgeous one," Ralph responded, his eyes warming.

"She's a good chit. Glad you've seen it's worth putting up with her annoying habits."

"You aren't supposed to admit she's got any. Remember we are newly married. I might not have discovered them as yet."

"I think you discovered them from the moment you met her," Miles said, remembering one of their early meetings, in which Ralph and Edith had argued.

"I went into my marriage with my eyes fully open," Ralph said with a shrug.

"I suppose I did too."

"You inadvertently picked a good wife," Ralph said gently.

"Yes. She is everything I could wish for," Miles replied.

"But?"

"The difficulty I have is that if I—"

The men were interrupted by the arrival of Lord Hoylake. He was a man prone to gambling and very often challenged Ralph to a card game or two. Ralph had used gaming as a way to block out the worry and concern he had for his mother. He'd found when concentrating on the way an opponent was going to play, he could think of nothing else. It had made him a formidable opponent to anyone who chose to play against him.

"Morning, my good fellows," Lord Hoylake said lazily. "Can I persuade you to join me in a game of vingt-et-un?" Both declined the offer, at which the gentleman looked askance at Ralph. "I'm surprised you can't be persuaded. Turned over a new leaf since you got leg-shackled, have you?"

"Yes," Ralph said. "I find the cards don't hold the same allure as my wife does."

Lord Hoylake grimaced. "Ah, it'll wear off, believe me. Probably in about three months."

"As he's married a prime article, I expect his distraction to last a little longer," Miles responded in defence of his sister.

"Will yours last as long?" Lord Hoylake asked Miles.

"I would expect so," Miles said, but with a little discomfort.

Watching Miles assessingly, Lord Hoylake flicked open his snuff box and took a pinch. "That bet surrounding your recent betrothal seemed a little havey-cavey to me."

"What do you mean by that?" Miles asked.

Lord Hoylake shrugged. "The odds didn't stack up."

"It doesn't matter now; it's old news," Ralph interjected.

"How do you mean, they didn't stack up?" Miles persisted.

"Let me recall. There were three possible husbands, but the odds against you were so low, it was almost as if the person setting the bet knew it would be you from the outset. Now, I'm not one for making accusations about fellow gentlemen, but even the most foolish wouldn't bet on such heavily weighted odds," Lord Hoylake explained.

157

"I never saw the odds," Miles said. He took out his snuff box from his pocket, his hand shook a little with the realisation of what Lord Hoylake was saying.

"I thought it was out of character for you to be involved, but someone close to you was trying to make a quick coin out of you, I feel. It was almost as if they knew the outcome before the bet had been placed. Which can't be right, can it?"

Ralph and Miles remained quiet. When Lord Hoylake realised he wasn't going to receive anything further from them, he shrugged. "Good day to you, gentlemen. I shall see if I can persuade another to indulge me in a hand or two."

It was a few moments before Miles spoke. "The bet was a false one."

"No it wasn't," Ralph said. "There was a bet raised here. Don't take any notice of Hoylake. He was just trying to get a rise out of you."

Miles stood. "I need to speak to someone about who placed the bet."

"Leave it, Miles. It won't achieve anything."

"You didn't do it, did you?"

"Don't be ridiculous. I wasn't even in town," Ralph said.

"Of course not. Good. That gives me some comfort. I find it odd that the person who created the bet weighted it in such a way. I need to find out what's going on. I'll return soon." Miles walked away.

Ralph groaned. This wasn't going to end happily.

*

Miles burst into the barracks at Hyde Park. On being told Jones was still in his rooms, he marched up the stairs and, without waiting for permission to enter, flung open the door and walked in, eyes blazing.

"You damned cur!"

"What the devil's got into you?" Jones's wary eyes belied his nonchalant drawl.

"Where's Dunn?" Miles demanded.

"On an errand for the king. Why?"

"Why? *Why*?" Miles shouted. "I want to kill you both, that's why!"

"Stop the dramatics, Longdon," Jones said. "You're hurting my ears."

Miles threw his body at Jones, toppling his friend over, along with the chair he'd been seated on. The two struggled, but others soon ran into the room, brought by the commotion, and quickly separated them.

After being cursed for acting like guttersnipes and threatened about creating any further disturbances, the pair assured everyone that there would be no repeat of such bad behaviour and were left alone.

"I should damn well call you out for what you've done," Miles said, his jaw tight.

"What? Caused you to marry a perfectly respectable, personable heiress? My heart bleeds for your hardship. It really does," Jones responded with derision.

"You had no right forcing to me to marry her." Miles straightened his frock coat, pulling roughly on the fabric.

Jones shrugged. "You could have refused."

"And see her ruined? I am not the type of man who could leave her to her fate."

"I would have," Jones admitted. He righted an upturned chair and sat on it.

"Yet you interfered."

"The poor chit is besotted with you. Why not give you a nudge when you didn't realise her feelings or your own? For I think you aren't as immune as you consider yourself, or even you wouldn't have agreed to tie yourself to Miss King."

"It wasn't your decision to make," Miles insisted.

"Perhaps not. But you wouldn't have realised you were affected by her if you hadn't been pushed."

"I wouldn't have married her only for the bet," Miles said, but his words caused deep feelings of guilt to crawl through his insides.

"Why? Has it been hell?" Jones asked, genuinely curious.

"No. She's no tabby. But that isn't the point."

"I think it is."

"I'll never forgive you for this," Miles said. "I thought I could trust you with my life. How wrong I was."

"You are not taking part in some Cheltenham tragedy," Jones mocked, folding his arms. "It seems I know you better than you do. If that causes a breech between us, I'm sorry for that, but I won't regret my actions. It was the right thing to do for you both."

"And you such a paragon. You have the gall to interfere in my life?" Miles spat.

"This isn't about me. It's about you being married to a girl you probably don't deserve. Go and treasure your wife, Miles, and appreciate what you have, instead of focusing on how cheated you feel. You are a lucky man, if only you'd realise it. Which, in my books, makes you mutton-headed, something I'd never thought you'd be."

Chapter 17

Susan waited in their shared sitting room, watching the food congeal and cool as she held back, hoping Miles would arrive as he'd promised when they'd parted that morning.

It had been wonderful, going to bed with him and falling asleep wrapped in his arms. They'd woken early, he'd kissed her into wakefulness before making love to her gently but passionately. Afterwards they'd enjoyed a leisurely breakfast in their sitting room, not wishing to be parted by the formality of the breakfast table.

Separating to do their daily duties, Miles had kissed Susan with a kiss so full of promise and tenderness that she'd needed his arms around her to remain standing. She could never have believed she could feel so happy.

Edith had stayed long after morning calls had finished, and it had been something special to be able to share some, although not all, of the delight she had found in being with Miles. As she was embraced by Edith before her friend had finally departed, Susan had felt that for the first time she was truly blessed.

Now, she was growing concerned at Miles's lateness. He wasn't the type of person not to send word if he'd changed his mind. Nibbling on a piece of bread, she rang the bell. There was no point in keeping the food any longer. It had spoiled and wasn't fit for consumption.

As the footman cleared the dishes, Susan asked if there had been any news from her husband.

"He returned home some time ago, m'lady, and has been in his study ever since with strict instructions he wasn't to be disturbed," the footman answered.

"Oh. Thank you," Susan said, trying to hide her surprise and disappointment.

She didn't react until the room was cleared. Only then did she move to the door leading to the landing. Something serious must have happened for Miles to lock himself away. She immediately went to help.

Susan knocked gently on the door; there was no response from inside. Only hesitating for a moment, Susan turned the handle and pushed the door open.

The fire was low in the grate, the curtains opened, although the night was dark outside. Miles was seated in one of the wing-back chairs, a glass in his hand and an almost empty decanter by his side.

Entering the room, Susan closed the door with a click, which Miles didn't acknowledge. She hurried over to him and crouched down by his side.

"Miles? What is it? What's happened?" she asked, touching his hand gently.

It took a moment for Miles to turn towards her, but he said nothing in answer to her questions, just taking a swig of liquid from his glass.

Susan gasped as she saw his eye was bruised and closing. "Your eye! Have you been attacked?"

"No. I attacked Jones," Miles finally answered, but his words were slurred.

"Captain Jones? Why ever would you do that?" There was something wrong. Susan began to feel an unaccountable sense of dread, but she had to persist in asking questions.

"He's a damned sneaksby, that's why," Miles answered.

"But you and he are such good friends."

"Ha! Not anymore. I never want to see his face again. Or Dunn's, or I'll beat him when I see him," Miles ranted drunkenly.

"Please tell me what's happened," Susan begged.

"The bet. That blasted bet."

Paling, Susan continued to push. "What about it?"

"They made the whole thing up. It wasn't real. Jones and Dunn arranged it when we returned to London."

Susan felt as if she'd been slapped. She sat on the wooden floor with a stifled sob. Blinking away her sudden tears, she forced herself to stand and move to the chair opposite Miles. He wouldn't have noticed her choked tone, but she swallowed until she was sure her voice would be steady enough to question him further.

"The bet about me?" she finally asked.

"Yes. They decided we were to marry and so forced our hand." Miles turned and filled his glass with the last of the liquid.

"I see," Susan said. "Why did they do that?"

"'Cause you liked me, and I'm an honourable fool."

Wincing, Susan nodded. "You are honourable, but you aren't a fool."

"Now, we're stuck with it."

"I thought we were happy these last few days," Susan said quietly. "I thought there was hope for us."

It seemed that Miles hadn't heard her, but when she thought she couldn't feel any worse, he took a drink and said, "I wanted to pick my own blasted wife in my own time.

163

If I were ever to marry at all. Instead the decision was bloody well forced on me."

Susan didn't say another word. She couldn't have done so. She ran out of the room, the door swinging back in her haste to leave the most hurtful words she'd ever heard behind.

Not caring which servants saw her, she ran up the stairs and into her chamber. She crawled into her bed, still fully clothed, and burrowed under the covers, sobbing and hiding from a very cruel world.

When eventually the tears stopped, she climbed off her bed. It was time to give him back his life.

Not ringing the bell, she grabbed her bonnet and reticule. She had to leave. And now.

*

Susan entered Florence's chamber with only slightly less speed than she'd exited her own. Florence looked at her niece from her dressing table looking-glass; she'd been preparing for bed, her hair being plaited by her maid. Her eyes widened in surprise as Susan crumpled at her feet and rested her head on Florence's lap with a sob.

Florence nodded to her maid to leave them alone. She waited until the door closed behind the servant before speaking. Resting her hand on Susan's head, she stroked it gently.

"Come. What is this? You aren't prone to hysterics. What's come over you to upset you so?" Florence asked.

"It's all been a farce! I'm going to be a laughing stock! And he hates me," Susan sobbed.

"Who hates you? And since when have you worried about such trifles?"

164

"Since my husband regrets marrying me!"

"I think you'd better tell me what's been going on," Florence said matter-of-factly. "My imagination is running riot, and it's usually not half as bad when the full story is known."

Susan sniffed. "I doubt you'll think that," she said, looking at her aunt.

"You, my dear, are a sight indeed. I hope to goodness no one saw you on your journey here. You look positively wild!"

Susan's eyes filled with further tears, but she wiped her face with her handkerchief and made an effort to straighten her hair. Her aunt guided her to the chaise longue and seated her gently.

"Tell me everything," Florence said. Listening to the whole sorry tale, she didn't interrupt until Susan came to an exhausted end.

"I can't remain in London. I don't want to face him. I can't see the regret or despair in his expression," Susan said, finally able to speak without tears.

"Those are very serious words, my dear. Are you sure you wish to abandon your home?" Florence asked.

"Yes, because I've never felt so desolate, and it was never truly my home." Susan scrunched her handkerchief into a tight ball. It was better to do that than release the wail of despair which filled her body.

"You are prepared to become estranged from the man you love and accept the exclusion from society that will follow as a consequence?"

"Yes. I'm only sorry I didn't seek out a solitary life prior to being married," Susan said. "I let my heart rule my head, and Miles has suffered because of it. I shouldn't have been selfish."

"You are the most unselfish girl a person could know, or you'd have abandoned your father years ago," Florence said. "Why you stayed to be browbeaten by that harridan I'll never know. She's done you untold damage."

Susan grimaced. "At this moment I feel as if every decision I've ever made has been a poor one."

"Now, now. Don't become a dramatic watering pot. You're better than that," Florence gently scolded.

"What do I do, Aunt? How can I stop this pain?"

"My first advice would be to return home and sort this out with your husband."

"I can't do that."

"You won't do that. There's a difference."

"I disagree, but you're stubborn, so there's no point in my arguing," Susan said with a sniff.

Florence smiled appreciatively. "In that case, get yourself off to your country home."

"But that belongs to Miles."

"Yes. As he holds your fortune now, tell me, what other plans did you have? You say you wish to abandon him, but how do you raise the funds to do so? I doubt my foolish brother will be allowed to spend anything further on you, if his doxy of a wife has any say in the matter."

Susan sagged. "I hadn't thought as far as funds."

"Of course you hadn't," came the damning response. "Get yourself off to Barrowfoot House. Spend some time away from London. Perhaps your husband will follow; maybe he won't. Being out of the glare of society will give you time to think properly. If then you decide you want to be estranged from your husband, you will have to hope he doesn't divorce you but settles an amount on you that you can live off," Florence said. She was businesslike, although not unkindly.

"He should be allowed to petition for a divorce, but I couldn't bear the scandal, and it would devastate Papa," Susan said. She walked to the window and looked blindly outside. Leaving him would destroy her whatever happened, but that was not of consideration. Miles's future was all that was important.

"I don't think Lord Longdon is the type to divorce. He seems a young man who takes his responsibilities seriously. Come, sit down."

"But this marriage was based on falsehoods. He can't be condemned for wishing for release. After all, it was through meddling by his friends, nothing to do with him or his wishes," Susan pointed out, obeying her aunt's request.

"Are his friends cruel? Or do you think they secretly dislike him?" Florence asked.

"No. Neither. In fact I would say they think very highly of him," Susan answered.

"Then what was their reason for embarking on such a prank? It would be a strange thing to do to someone you liked without there being a reason behind it. I don't think we know their motivation, which could shed some light on your predicament."

"Whatever it is, Miles has made it clear he regrets being forced into marriage with me. How we reached that position is irrelevant. I need to release him in the only way I can," Susan said, finally sounding stronger.

"If that is your decision, do as I say, and if he isn't generous with some sort of settlement, let me know and I will support you," Florence said.

"I couldn't become a drain on your resources!" Susan said hotly.

"You are going to inherit my wealth at some point. This will mean you are just receiving some of it a little early."

Florence shrugged. "Keeping you isn't going to cause me any hardship, I can assure you."

"It's the principle of the action. I know you aren't a pauper." Susan gave her aunt a small smile.

"That's better. You are far prettier when you smile. Crying makes your nose red and your skin blotchy. I wouldn't use it to try to win an argument, my dear. Leave that to the women who can cry daintily."

"I shall take note," Susan said, her lips twitching.

"Good girl. Now, are you sending a note for your portmanteau and maid, or shall I?" Florence asked.

"I shall," Susan said. "I also want to take Billy with me." She moved to the small writing desk in the corner of the room.

"Billy? Is that a new horse?"

"No. He's a young boy who cared for me when I was on the ship. I persuaded Miles to have him released from his position and take him into his own household. I won't leave him under Miles's care. I know he would be honourable, but I feel Billy is my responsibility," Susan explained.

"I think your logic is misplaced, but you'll do as you wish," Florence said. "Don't plan on travelling tomorrow. Get an early start the day after."

"No. I shall leave first thing in the morning. There is no point delaying," Susan said firmly.

"It would give you time to speak to—"

"It's too late for that," Susan interrupted. "Better to leave as soon as possible."

Chapter 18

The noise was deafening. Miles moaned, but that seemed to increase the sound and the throbbing inside his head. Trying to open his eyes, he winced as they reacted to the light in the room.

"Close the curtains," he groaned.

"They are closed, my lord. It's the middle of the night," Ashurst said quietly.

"Good God, my head," Miles said, his pale, clammy skin turning a sickly green colour. "I think I need–"

Ashurst was already standing next to the bed with a bowl in readiness for the result of too much alcohol and an extremely disturbed night.

It was some time before Miles flopped back on the bed.

"My lord, your drink. You need to try it to ease the headache," Ashurst coaxed.

Grimacing, Miles moaned again. "No. Not yet."

Accepting that the liquid would probably reappear as fast as Miles drank it, the valet got rid of the bowl before returning with a jug of cool water and cloths to wipe his master's hot, sweaty brow.

Miles had fallen back into a fitful sleep, but at the valet's ministrations, he woke again. "Susan?" he croaked.

"Lady Longdon isn't here at the moment, my lord," Ashurst replied.

"She makes the headaches go," Miles said, but he was barely awake.

Ashurst's face betrayed none of the relief he felt at not needing to offer any further explanation. It was going to be a difficult conversation when the time came. He wasn't aware what had gone on between master and mistress, but one thing he knew for definite was that he'd not seen Miles as bad as this since Waterloo. And that didn't bode well for any of them.

*

Miles opened his eyes slightly. He'd not felt as ill as this in a long time. His whole body ached, and the thud in his head would be spectacular if it weren't so damned painful. Forcing his eyes open, he was relieved to note that it was still dark outside; at least that would help in his struggle to look around.

Ashurst was nearby, watching his master closely. Slowly looking around the room, Miles felt a stab of disappointment that Susan wasn't there.

"Are you ready for your drink, my lord?" Ashurst asked quietly.

"Yes. I hope so, because I can't stand this level of pain for much longer," Miles whispered.

Without another sound, Ashurst helped Miles to raise his head enough to swallow the liquid. Miles thought he was going to cast up his accounts once more at the movement, but after a few slow breaths he managed to ease the nausea enough to drink.

Lying back on the pillow with a sigh of relief, he closed his eyes. He could do no more. Before he fell into a fitful sleep, he asked one question. "Susan?"

"Lady Longdon isn't available at the moment," came Ashurst's reply.

A frown creased Miles's brow at the answer, but he didn't utter another sound.

*

"My mouth feels like the inside of an unkempt stable," Miles groaned, waking the following evening. "What on earth is amiss with me?"

"Ah, a full decanter and a severe night," Ashurst explained.

Miles groaned again. "I vaguely remember something."

"I'm sure it will come back to you. It usually does."

"You fiend. You'd have me believe I do this every week," Miles cursed good-naturedly, but he still spoke barely above a whisper.

"No. Not since the last battle," Ashurst said gently. He had been Miles's batman throughout all of his campaigns.

"That was justified." Quietly resting for a moment, Miles thought back over the previous days. He grimaced when he remembered his interview with Jones. He turned to Ashurst. "The nightmares haven't been as bad the last two times I've suffered."

"No." Ashurst looked uncomfortable.

"Do you think it's the drink that caused this episode to be worse than normal?"

"No."

"Speak, man! It's clear you have something on your mind, and I haven't the wherewithal to coax it out of you!" Miles exclaimed.

171

Ashurst coughed with embarrassment. "If you'd permit me to say, my lord, Lady Longdon was not with you this time."

"How would that affect it?"

"From the little I saw, you seemed to respond to her soothing. As if you were brought out of the nightmare even though you didn't wake," Ashurst said. "I might be wrong, for I didn't remain long in the room when she assured me she wished to care for you."

"I didn't realise you'd left her. I'd presumed you'd both been in attendance for the first part of the night at least," Miles said. Memories of waking up with Susan in his arms flitted into his mind. "Did you instruct her on what to do?"

"No. She seemed to know instinctively what would help. The only instruction I gave her was when to give you your drink when you awoke."

"I didn't feel I needed it the second time she was with me," Miles said. No. He'd been so focused on a far more enjoyable exploration of his new wife to have barely thought about the potion he always took. It was only later that he'd actually drunk it, and that was at her instigation. He'd never not taken the stuff after suffering a nightmare previously.

The valet thought it prudent to busy himself whilst his master pondered the realisation of what and who had helped more than anyone or anything since he'd returned from the war.

"Where is my wife now?" Miles eventually asked.

"I'm not quite sure," Ashurst admitted truthfully, although he, along with the other senior members of staff, knew at least some of what had gone on. "I have been with you during last night and today."

"It's an early hour, is it not?" Miles asked. "Has she gone out?"

"It's almost ten of the clock in the evening. You've been out of things a full night and a day. You have taken a while to return to us."

Miles frowned. "Ashurst, where is my wife?"

"I'm afraid I don't know."

"But," Miles prompted.

"She has visited her aunt."

"What am I not realising?" Miles demanded, lifting himself to a seated position. "Tell me the truth."

"You have had some sort of altercation with Captain Jones, if your mumblings are to be believed," Ashurst said, distinctly uncomfortable. "When you came home, you went to your study and remained there. Lady Longdon joined you at some point but soon returned to her chamber. She then left for her aunt's abode."

Miles put his head in his hands. "The bet. The bloody bet," he groaned as memories reappeared with uncomfortable speed.

Ashurst clearly thought it prudent to remain silent.

Eventually, Miles looked at his valet. "Have you any inkling what I said to her?" There was no point trying to tiptoe around the situation. He'd erred, and he needed to know how badly.

"No. Although I'm led to believe she was distressed when she left you."

"Dear God, what have I done?" Miles said. "I need to visit her aunt."

"Now, my lord? I would advise that a call in the morning would be more appropriate."

"But this happened yesterday."

173

"I would still suggest you visit in the morning, for the sake of gossip, if nothing else," Ashurst said. "But there is something else you need to be aware of."

"Go on," Miles said, apprehension building.

"Lady Longdon sent for her portmanteau, her maid and the boy."

"Then I have hurt her deeply," Miles said. "Damn the consequences, get me dressed. I'm going out."

Chapter 19

Susan had set off a little later than she'd intended. Her aunt had tried to persuade her to remain in order to speak to Miles, but Susan had been steadfast in her refusal.

"Aunt, there is nothing to be gained in my remaining with him," Susan said, more focused than she had ever been. "It's time, for probably the first time in my life, that I put my fate in my own hands."

"That's something, I suppose," Aunt Florence sniffed. "When you've decided what you're doing, let me know. I will be following you, my dear."

"There's no need for you to uproot your life," Susan insisted.

"You're the only thing that's precious to me in this life. I shall be attached to your tails whether you disappear to Scotland, Italy, or beyond. You might as well get used to the thought of my being with you because, like you, I won't be dissuaded."

Susan kissed her aunt. "I don't deserve you. Thank you."

"You deserve a loving husband and a family in which you could flourish and shake off what has happened in the past. I'm very disappointed that Lord Longdon didn't come up to par. I had high hopes for him," Aunt Florence said.

"It was the circumstances. We were both foolish to try to make it work." Susan tried to sound pragmatic, but the lead weight in her heart gave her eyes a distraught look. "It's time I left."

She was using her aunt's carriage. Billy and her maid were inside already, waiting for their mistress to enter. With one last embrace and the promise of writing soon, Susan entered the carriage and, as she waved goodbye, the equipage set off.

"I'm sorry for removing you from your post so soon after settling you in, Billy. But I feel you are my charge and responsibility," Susan explained when the lump in her throat had been swallowed.

"It's another adventure, my lady," Billy responded with a smile. "I'm happy to be wherever you are."

"I'm glad to hear that."

"Are we to stay at Barrowfoot for a while, my lady?" Jane, her maid, asked.

Susan was fully aware that her lifelong retainer would have something to say when they were in the privacy of a bedchamber; she could only be thankful that her maid clearly didn't wish Billy to hear the chiding that would be coming Susan's way.

"We'll be there for at least a few days. I'm not sure as yet," Susan said honestly. She had no idea how long it would take Miles to follow her; part of her hoped he wouldn't. Not having the torture of seeing him again would be preferable, although her heart ached for it to be otherwise.

The three travellers didn't speak much, other than when Billy exclaimed at some sight or other. Susan found out he'd been a foundling and thought his dreams had been answered when he'd been apprenticed to his captain. As the journey progressed he saw much to delight him, acting as a younger child would in his wonderment.

If Billy's rescue was to be the only good thing to come out of her recent escapades, Susan couldn't be sorry about the result. Protecting him from cruelty would have to be enough satisfaction for her. She refused to dwell on anything else.

*

Florence remained seated when Miles was shown into her drawing room. Her expression showed nothing but contempt for the peer who had let her niece down so much.

Miles bowed before her and started to speak. "I'm here to have a private word with my wife. I'm led to believe she is has taken up temporary residence here."

"She's not available. In fact, even if she were, she's decided that she wants nothing more to do with you," Florence said coldly.

Miles couldn't hide the wince at the words, before he schooled his features once more. "Please. I have been a buffoon of the highest order. I understand she would wish me to the devil, but I need to explain my actions to Susan."

"And what would be achieved by that? Are you going to try to withdraw the comments you've made?"

"No. I can't do that. But I can apologise for them," Miles answered.

"And do you think apologising will magically rub them away? What could possibly convince my niece that you are happy to have her as your wife when you've told her that you're not?"

Miles sat heavily on a chair. "I didn't say that, did I?" he asked, anguished.

Florence frowned at him. "Do you not remember what you said?"

"It's not completely clear, I admit."

"You blasted fool!"

"Yes. I am."

"You told her you wanted to be able to choose your own wife. That you were angry you'd been forced into a marriage with her. Which for a girl like Susan is probably the most cutting comment you could have made. You've rejected her in the worst possible way for someone who has suffered the abuse and undermining that she has. The poor chit," Florence explained, her words not quite as abrasive as they had been.

"Damn my foolishness!" Miles cursed. "I never intended to hurt her."

"Perhaps not, but you did."

"Yes. But now I want to make it better."

Sighing, Florence picked at her dress before speaking. "I know you had a rough start and perhaps wouldn't have chosen my niece if all things had been equal."

"No," Miles admitted.

"But, seriously ask yourself this. What else would you want from a wife?"

"I don't really understand."

"Think of what Susan brings to your marriage, and decide where she is lacking," Florence said.

Silence descended between them. Miles seemed to sag in his seat. Finally he looked at the older woman. "I already knew before I arrived here that there is nothing I'd change about Susan."

"So, you aren't a complete blockhead. I suppose that's something."

"Thank you," Miles said dryly.

"Oh, don't think you are out of the woods yet," Florence replied. "After all, you say that you'd not change my niece, yet you acted as if you disliked her at best." She was watching Miles closely, assessing him openly.

"I've been an utter fool. Not seeing what's under my nose and in my heart," Miles said. "Please allow me to speak to her and explain."

"I'm not stopping you, but Susan is."

"I don't understand."

"No. You wouldn't. My blasted sister-in-law has convinced Susan that she's worthless. That only someone wishing to obtain her fortune would consider marrying her. Certainly not the man she loved."

"She was in love with someone?" Miles asked, his heartbeat pounding uncomfortably.

"Oh yes. Completely besotted. But he didn't want her," Florence said, watching Miles as she had the few times they'd met. "When the kidnap situation and your marriage occurred, I thought there was hope for her. You seemed a decent sort, and I foolishly hoped that fondness would lead to love. It appears it hasn't, and by rejecting Susan so cruelly, you may have done irrevocable harm"

"In what way?"

"She's decided that her fate will be no longer at anyone else's mercy. She is going to live her life not as she would wish, but in a way where she won't risk getting hurt again."

"That sounds very final," Miles said, leaning forward and clasping his hands.

"It sounds a very lonely life to me."

"She could give me a second chance," Miles said hopefully.

"And let you break her heart a second time?"

"I realise I've caused her distress, but …"

"She's been in love with you for years. You never noticed, thereby rejecting her the first time. Now, you have rejected her a second time in a quite spectacular way. How much more do you expect her to withstand?" Florence asked sharply.

Rubbing his hands over his face, Miles looked at Florence. "I suspected it. No. I knew it. Deep down anyway, I knew she had feelings for me. I've been an idiot, and I need to make amends. One thing is for sure: I can't leave her believing that I don't care for her, for I do. I care for her very much."

"I hope so, for she is worth your affection. In fact she's worth ten of you."

"You won't hear any arguments to the contrary from me," Miles responded quickly. "Please let me see her." He was leaning forward in his seat, his hands reaching out as if in a silent appeal.

"She's not here."

"Has she gone out?"

"She left for your country home this morning. Just before luncheon. I suggest you follow her as soon as you are able," Florence said. "I know she doesn't wish for you to seek her out, but I think it would be for the best."

"She doesn't wish to see me?" His body moved back as if struck by the realisation that he might have lost Susan.

"Would you wish to torture yourself further? Despite her upbringing, she is one of the most loving people anyone could wish to meet. Give her some credit, though, for reaching the end of her tether. Her heart is battered."

"She has given me nothing but affection and care. I need to show her that I'm worthy of her regard. I shall leave first thing in the morning," Miles said, standing.

"I hope you don't let her down this time. If you do there will be no return from it, for either of you," Florence warned.

"I will not fail her. Not now, nor in the future." With a bow, Miles left the room.

*

Susan couldn't face breakfast. She hadn't anticipated how much it would affect her to stay in the same inn as she had on her last trip to Barrowfoot House with Miles. She'd almost refused the private parlour, but then common sense had made her act appropriately.

Deciding to take a short walk, she smiled at Billy, who was watching the ostlers attach the horses to the carriage with fascination.

As she left the inn yard, she paused and breathed in a lungful of morning air. She'd felt constrained in the carriage, needing to maintain some level of decorum when she'd have liked to wallow in self-pity.

Turning to walk down the lane, she stopped in her tracks. "Oh no. No. No. It can't be."

Mr. Sage grinned, despite his bedraggled attire, and bowed his head slightly in mock greeting. "Why, Lady Longdon, fancy meeting you here," he said, pointing his pistol at Susan's midriff.

"How did you survive?" Susan asked.

"There was a ledge." Mr. Sage shrugged. "No one looked underneath it, all running around and focusing on the water. The fools. If one of them had looked up, I'd have been seen. Once we set off on the journey, it was easy to climb aboard. The captain thought it a great joke to be taking money off the quality while hiding the man they

181

wanted dead. Just think, for the whole journey, I was but a few feet from you. Did you enjoy your afternoons on deck?"

Taking a sharp intake of breath, Susan tried to dampen down her panic. He was here, and she had no idea how she was going to get herself out of this situation. "How did you find me?"

"Oh, I've been in your vicinity ever since we returned to London. You've been too smitten with your new husband to notice an old beggar on the streets. You've even thrown me a penny or two." Mr. Sage smiled at her. "I did wonder how I was going to separate you from your entourage, but it seemed you played into my hands. Had an argument, did you? Fallen out with your beloved lord?"

"What do you want from me?" Susan asked, ignoring his questions. Her insides were cold with the thought she'd been followed so openly and she hadn't noticed a thing. How had she noticed Mr. Malone watching her and yet not Mr. Sage? She had to acknowledge that Sage was right; her infatuation with Miles had made her blind to everything around her.

"It would seem that I can't access your fortune, for I doubt I could persuade your father to file for an annulment of the marriage," Mr. Sage said conversationally. It would have seemed a pleasant exchange only for the weapon he held.

"No," Susan said with a slight blush to her cheeks.

"So the honourable lord has bedded the plain spinster. Wonders will never cease," Mr. Sage said.

"My husband has my fortune. I can't be of use to you anymore."

"Ah, but that's the thing. He would pay for your safe return – he wouldn't want the death of his wife on his conscience, I'm sure."

182

"You are kidnapping me a second time?" Susan asked, incredulous. Even she could see the ridiculousness of the situation.

"This time I won't be relying on Malone," Mr. Sage sneered. "Come, my high and mighty lady. Your carriage awaits, and we are going to take it."

Susan's maid took that moment to walk around the corner, in search of her mistress. Stifling a scream, she came to a halt.

Mr. Sage looked at her. "Perfect timing. Go and clear everyone away from your coach, and your mistress will live. We are going on a little journey."

Jane was rooted to the spot, and Susan saw a flicker of annoyance pass over Mr. Sage's face. She knew he had nothing to lose. Everyone nearby was in real danger. "Jane, do as he says. Tell the staff I want no heroics. I don't want anyone to get hurt on my account."

"Now!" Mr. Sage bellowed at Jane before she had time to answer Susan's words.

With a sob, Jane ran back the way she came. Mr. Sage gave her a few moments to implement his instructions before he waved his pistol to make Susan move. "Come, let's get this started," he said, walking her back to the inn.

Using Susan as a shield, he shouted at everyone standing in the yard, "No one try to save her and she'll live, for now. Anyone foolish enough to try to rescue her will cause her to die. Instantly. Do I make myself clear?"

A few nods were received at his words and although they were watched closely, no one made a move while Susan and Mr. Sage made their way to the carriage.

Susan stopped at the carriage door, but Mr. Sage pressed the gun into her back. "Not this time. There will be no jumping out of carriages for you. I learned from your friend not to give any woman the opportunity to escape. However slight. You'll sit up front with me."

Struggling with shaking legs, Susan climbed the steps at the front of the vehicle and seated herself quickly. Mr. Sage climbed up with hardly any difficulty while using only one hand.

"You're a competent horsewoman. You take the reins," he instructed, putting the gun to her ribs. "No hitting holes in the road in the hope you'll unseat me. This pistol will go off if there are any sudden movements from me."

Susan did as she was bid. As she gave one last glimpse at Jane, she wondered where Billy was. She could only be thankful he wasn't in the yard. She couldn't have him trying to protect her as he had on the ship.

Watching behind them for a while to make sure they weren't being followed, Mr. Sage didn't say anything, leaving Susan to drive the team of four at a rapid pace. When he was satisfied they were alone, he started to give instructions.

"Turn off this road at the next signpost. We won't be following the main routes."

"This is a large carriage. It will hardly fit if you take us down the country lanes," Susan said.

"Thankfully, the care of the carriage is not my concern. Not leaving an easy trail is. I won't have that husband of yours performing heroics a second time."

"He won't. I can guarantee that. He regrets marrying me. He'll probably refuse to pay the ransom, enabling him to get rid of the wife he doesn't want," Susan said dully, dutifully turning the horses down a narrower, more rutted lane. Her aunt's fine animals would not be impressed with where she was guiding them.

"If he doesn't pay, your father will," Mr. Sage said confidently.

Susan thought it prudent not to mention that her father wouldn't do anything without her stepmother's say-so, so that avenue of exploitation could be as tricky as approaching Miles. She concentrated on trying to avoid the deeper ruts, whilst Mr. Sage gave her more instructions and urged her to maintain a good speed.

"Unless you wish to bring this journey to an early halt, you'll allow me to drive the horses in a way which will get them and us to wherever you intend in a timely manner," Susan said primly.

"You are a cursed baggage!" Mr. Sage snarled.

Susan flinched at the way his empty hand fisted, expecting a blow, but it didn't come. She decided she would try to memorise her route and concentrate on extracting herself from her predicament as soon as it was safe to do so. One thing was for sure: she could rely on no one else to save her. If she was to have a future, it depended on her own actions.

Chapter 20

Jones and Dunn arrived at Curzon Street first thing in the morning. Jones's expression was thunderous. "This is a fool's errand," he grumbled as Dunn knocked on the door.

"I'm not spending the next six months watching over my shoulder and expecting Longdon to jump out at me at any moment. If he wants to have it out about the bet, better on my terms. He's always more forgiving in the morning when he's barely woken up," Dunn said.

On opening the door, the butler informed the men that his lordship was about to embark on a journey and wasn't available to see visitors.

"Oh, let me in, man!" Dunn exclaimed, his frayed nerves breaking. "I have to get this over with today." Pushing past the butler, both men entered the hallway to a hive of activity.

Miles walked out of this study, pulling on his gloves, and halted when he saw who was in the hallway. "I said no visitors," he said to the butler.

"Don't blame him. Dunn pushed his way in in his own brutish way," Jones said in his usual lazy tone.

"I haven't the time to deal with you now," Miles snapped. "I don't actually want to see either of you again."

"Told you not to panic," Jones said to Dunn.

Flashing his friend a look, Dunn stepped forward. "Look. I'm here to apologise. It was a bloody foolish scheme, and I want to make amends."

"It's too late for that," Miles said brusquely.

"Miles, you aren't usually such a bull-calf. Come on, we can resolve this," Dunn appealed to his friend.

Sighing, Miles shook his head as if in resignation. "Come into my study," he said, turning on his heel and walking back through the door he'd just come through.

Jones and Dunn followed and closed the door behind them.

"Is something amiss?" Jones asked immediately.

"You could say that," Miles said tightly. "I stupidly got roaring bosky after finding out about the bet, and my wife, coming to me in all concern, was told what I thought was the truth about my situation, which has resulted in her leaving me."

"Have you got windmills in your head?" Jones asked in disbelief. "It's the only thing that would explain your actions."

"As you were the one who started this whole blasted farce, I'd watch my mouth if I were you," Miles responded.

"Boys. There can be no gain in going over old ground," Dunn said, forever the peacemaker. "What we need to know is how you are going to make amends."

"I was trying to do that when you arrived. Apparently, she's travelling to Barrowfoot. I intend to follow her; in fact, I'd be on the road now, only you're delaying me."

"In that case, there is no time to lose," Dunn said, opening the door. "A good thing we came on our horses. Come, we'll set out immediately."

"*We*?" Miles asked incredulously.

"Of course," Jones replied. "You don't expect us to trust you to solve this on your own, do you? Now, before you waste even more time by arguing with us, don't be an obstinate pig. As much as it pains me to admit, we have erred, and if needed we shall relay that fact to Lady Longdon. If she doesn't forgive you after that, we shall use our abilities to throw you off your estate, for our loyalties lie with her, of course."

"Of course," Miles said, with a shake of his head. He walked into the hallway, nodding to his valet. "Follow me down at a reasonable pace. I have all I need for the few days on the road, and now it seems I am to have company." He nodded in the direction of the two captains.

"We shall right what has been wronged," Jones said. "Come, Longdon. Now is not the time for long goodbyes with your staff. We have a lady to find!"

*

"Where are we headed? Do we just ride until the horses drop dead?" Susan asked, her tone not completely hiding the sarcasm in her voice.

They had been travelling for some time down lanes that seemed to lead to nowhere. Apart from the occasional farm, there had been no buildings on their journey, and other than a few cows, sheep and an occasional interested horse, they had not met a soul. It was looking more unlikely that even if Susan managed to escape that she would find anyone to help her.

"You do as I say. You'll live longer that way," Mr. Sage snapped.

Susan grimaced and wriggled in her seat. "Seriously, I need to know for practical reasons."

"Damn it! Why can't you just sit and be silent?"

"Because the call of nature is becoming more pressing." Susan shrugged. "If I know we are to stop soon, I can wait, but not for much longer."

"I haven't seen anything suitable as yet, so it may be some time," Mr. Sage said.

Susan turned to him in surprise. "You haven't planned this out?"

"Mind your own damned business!"

"You are relying on us finding an unused building, aren't you? This is what this rambling journey is about. I foolishly thought it was to do with not leaving a trail, but it isn't. How could you embark on something so serious without thinking it through?" Susan demanded.

She didn't see his fist move until it connected with her jaw. She lurched backwards in her seat, letting go of the reins, arms flailing to try to grasp anything to prevent her falling off the coachman's seat. Mr Sage grabbed her roughly. Susan's fall was slowed although not stopped as he struggled to keep hold of her at the angle her body had slipped to.

Tumbling from approximately ten feet high was always going to hurt. Landing with a thud, Susan struggled to breathe, before losing consciousness on the dusty ground. The last thing she saw was Mr. Sage's muddy boots landing next to her as he jumped from the seat with a curse.

*

Miles, Jones and Dunn made good progress. They didn't travel at the speed that their trip to the north had warranted, but they were men of action and used to travelling large distances faster than everyday riders were inclined to attempt.

Greatcoats securely around their bodies, scarves covering their faces, they presented an intimidating picture as they rode three abreast.

"We'll stop at the village I stayed at the last time I travelled down with Susan," Miles said as they neared the inn. "It's the only time she's done the journey, so I'm presuming she would have kept to the same route."

"Are you ready to beg forgiveness for your stupidity?" Jones asked.

"Are you?" Miles retorted.

"We are. Especially if it helps your cause," Dunn interjected, flashing a warning glance at Jones.

"It's very tedious when you don't let me have my fun," Jones said.

"We're not going to interfere, just apologise and support," Dunn insisted.

"Spoilsport," Jones groaned.

"At last one of you is talking sense, and I'm not referring to you," Miles said, looking at Jones.

"Married life is making you as tame as the rest of them. I'm glad I'll never agree to join the hallowed institution," Jones said.

Dunn grinned. "Famous last words, if ever I heard them."

"You wouldn't like to have a little bet on it, would you?" Jones retorted.

Miles growled, but Dunn shook his head. "You're an insensitive cad."

"It's one of my many talents," Jones answered with a grin.

"Please let me punch him before we enter the inn," Miles begged as they turned into the busy inn yard.

"Be nice," Dunn said.

Miles jumped from the saddle, not betraying the stiffness he felt from covering so many miles in only a few hours. After handing his horse to an ostler, he entered the inn and accepted a tankard of ale from the landlord.

"Has Lady Longdon left on her journey already?" Miles asked.

"Lord Longdon?" the innkeeper asked, looking uncomfortable.

"Yes," Miles answered, alert to the man's demeanour.

"I didn't recognise you at first, my lord. I think you should come into a private parlour," the innkeeper said, moving from behind the bar.

Jones and Dunn had entered the inn, ducking their heads to fit under the low doorway. "Is she here?" Dunn asked.

"There seems to be a problem," Miles said quietly, following the landlord.

The three men entered the room. The landlord turned to face them. He was pale and obviously discomfited.

"I'd like to start by saying nothing like this has ever happened before. I keep a good house, and the man in question hadn't stayed here," the man babbled, wishing that the three men facing him didn't look quite so ready to spring into action, for he knew his words would cause upset.

"What's happened to my wife?" Miles asked quietly.

"I can get her staff, if you like …"

"Tell me what you know, then I'll speak to the servants," Miles interrupted.

"There was an incident outside when the party were due to leave."

"What kind of an incident?" Jones asked.

191

"A man – I've no idea who he is – took Lady Longdon," the innkeeper confessed, his brow glistening with sweat. It would not do well for business when it was made known that a kidnapping had taken place on his premises.

"Took her? No one stopped him?" Miles asked incredulously.

"He had a gun. He swore he would shoot her if anyone attempted to rescue her. We didn't want her to be injured," the landlord tried to explain.

"Bloody cowards," Jones cursed.

Miles rubbed his hands over his face, trying to prevent the panic he felt overtaking him. "When did this happen?"

"This morning. About nine of the clock."

"That's hours ago! Get the servants who saw anything to come and speak to us. One at a time, but they'd best be quick. I want no hesitation in answering our questions – time is of the essence," Miles commanded.

The landlord left the room, and Miles sat heavily on a chair. Jones walked over to the fireplace, roughly picking up a poker and stabbing the logs on the fire viciously. Dunn remained fixed to his place.

"It can only be one person," Dunn said, breaking the silence.

"We couldn't find him. If he'd survived, we'd have found him," Jones said roughly.

"We presumed too much," Dunn responded quietly. "Accepting he would most likely have sunk in the mud made us lax."

"It might not be him," Jones said, not believing the words he uttered.

"Who else would want to harm her?" Miles asked.

"Damn it!" Jones exploded. "What can he want with her? He must know she's married."

"For all the good it's done her," Miles said with derision. "Where was I when she needed me most? Getting over a thumping head because I'd drunk myself into oblivion when I was behaving like a petulant child."

His two friends didn't have time to offer a response before a knock on the door indicated that the first witness to events had arrived.

Half an hour later everyone had been questioned, and the three were alone once more.

"It's him," Miles said dully.

"Yes. There can be no doubt," Dunn replied. No one had known Mr. Sage, but the description of him was clear and consistent.

"He's going to be desperate. How the hell are we to find her?" Miles asked.

Jones rested his hand on his friend's shoulder. "We will find her if we have to travel down every lane and road this county has to offer. We'll look at the more remote places, for he wouldn't want the risk of her gaining help from anyone seeing a lady in distress."

"They harmed her the last time," Miles said dully.

"We'll get to her before it comes to that." Dunn stood. "Come, we have some ground to cover. We'll stay together but separate briefly when we reach forks in the roads. There's no point going in three different directions. And we know the route the carriage set off on."

"They could have changed direction," Miles pointed out, but he was pulling his gloves on in preparation for leaving.

"Anyone passing them would remember a lady driving a carriage and four. We'll target the farm tracks first of all," Dunn said.

The three walked out of the inn and climbed onto the horses, which were already prepared for them. Miles nodded to the innkeeper. "I hope to be returning some time later. Please have three rooms in readiness."

"Yes, my lord," the innkeeper replied.

"We'll also be bringing back a dead body," Miles said grimly, failing to notice the paling of the landlord's features.

Chapter 21

Susan awoke to an insistent voice. It had been bothering the blackness that had enfolded her, and she was reluctant to let go. The voice persisted, though. It was like a fly buzzing around her, and she wanted to wave it away. Eventually accepting that she would have to open her eyes to make the noise stop, she slowly blinked, trying to focus.

"Oh, thank goodness! Please, my lady, wake up!" the voice persisted.

"What happened?" Susan croaked.

"I need to move you. You're on a dusty road," the voice answered urgently, ignoring her question.

"Billy?" Susan blinked at the unfocused face that hovered over her, its expression full of concern.

"Yes, my lady," Billy answered, almost crying with relief.

"What are you doing here? Am I back at the inn?" Susan asked, not attempting to move.

"No. You fell off the coachman's seat. I thought you were dead for a moment."

"You must think me very stupid," Susan said, and then frowned. "Billy, get to safety. Mr. Sage has a gun, and he'll use it."

Billy smiled slightly. "I've got his gun. He won't do anything."

The words spurred Susan to force herself to move, even though she felt very woozy and stiff. "Billy, can you help me to stand?"

The young boy moved and, gently pulling her hands, helped to lift her into a sitting position. Susan let go of the support Billy's hands were providing and placed her own firmly on the ground to steady herself.

"I feel a little dizzy," she admitted. "I think it's better if I don't move any further just at the moment. Please tell me what's been going on."

Billy needed no further encouragement. "I was hiding in the carriage, m'lady," he said, unable to keep the excitement from his voice. "I saw Mr. Sage walk around the corner with you, and I knew he'd be up to no good, so I climbed into the carriage. No one noticed me because they were all watching him with you."

"Oh, Billy, you do seem to be too willing to put yourself in danger on my account," Susan said.

"I couldn't leave you, m'lady. Not when you rescued me from the *Dolphin*," Billy responded seriously. "I thought I'd just be with you in the carriage, but then Mr. Sage made you drive the horses."

"Yes. I hadn't expected that either."

"I didn't know what I was going to do to help you, so I searched the carriage for weapons."

"I doubt my aunt carries weapons around with her," Susan said dryly.

"No she doesn't, but she does carry bricks for warming her feet. There was two under the seats," Billy said, a note of pride in his voice. "I took them out and put them next to me. I hadn't worked out how, but I knew I could use them."

"Oh, Billy, you will get yourself killed one of these days," Susan said gently. "You can't use a brick against a pistol."

"But he didn't know I was there," Billy pointed out, not unreasonably. "When you fell, I nearly gave myself away, I admit, but I managed to stop myself from shouting out. Mr. Sage ranted at you when you were on the ground. He even kicked you at one point."

Susan grimaced. "That doesn't surprise me, and it explains why my side is sore."

"I think he was going to carry you over and lift you into the carriage. He shoved his gun in his breeches and walked over to the carriage. I thought he was going to discover me, so I got one of the bricks. Instead, he just flung open the door and turned away. I thought I had to act then and there."

"My goodness!"

"It's fine. I'm light on my feet, so I jumped out of the carriage and hit him hard over the back of his head with the brick. He hadn't a clue what had happened. I've never seen someone drop to the floor like he did."

"Is he dead?" Susan asked in alarm. She didn't want Billy in trouble because he was trying to help.

"No. I thought he was, but he was still breathing, although not very hard. I took his gun and I've tied him up," Billy said proudly. "I couldn't drag him into the carriage, he's too heavy, but he's next to the door."

"It seems you have the whole situation under control." Susan smiled at her saviour. "I owe you my gratitude yet again. How am I ever going to repay you for this?"

Blushing, Billy smiled back. "I don't want paying, my lady. I just did what anyone would do."

197

"There were a lot of people in the inn yard," Susan said. "I don't condemn them for their inaction, as I probably would have been shot, but only you reacted to the situation I was in and came to my rescue in what seems to be a spectacular way. Don't underestimate what you've done. You were very brave."

If Billy was besotted with Susan before her speech, he was completely smitten by the end of it. He beamed at her bashfully.

Susan smiled in return. "I think I'd be able to stand now, if you could help me," she said, reaching out her hands for his.

Billy helped her to her feet, and although she needed to hold on to him and the side of the carriage for a few moments, she was able to remain upright.

"Let's see if Mr. Sage is still unconscious," she said, using the carriage for support as she walked around it to reach the other side.

Sage's body was lying where Billy had left it, beside the open carriage door. Susan used her foot to prod his prone form. She didn't wish for the dizziness to return if she bent forward to check him. She tensed as her foot touched his body, half expecting him to react, but there was no movement. Noticing Billy's handiwork of tying Sage's hands and feet with what looked to be a leather strap, she relaxed a little. It seemed she was in no immediate danger.

"We need to return to the inn, or some other place in which we could get help, but I'm going to struggle to climb into the driver's seat. Do you think you'd be able to drive the horses?" she asked.

"I ain't ever done that," Billy said doubtfully.

"They are very well behaved," Susan coaxed. "And they are probably a little tired now so won't be inclined to complain at your inexperienced hands. I'm sure you could do it. You are very capable."

"I'd have to turn the carriage around. How do I do that?"

"I think we'd best continue until we reach a turning in the road. These lanes would make the best of horsemen struggle. I wouldn't wish to cause you or the horses difficulty," Susan said gently. It would make their return journey longer because they couldn't try to follow the route back, but she spoke the truth. It would be too much to try to turn around in the small lanes they'd been travelling along.

"If you think I could …"

"I know you could. We both know you are very capable," Susan assured him. "Shall we try to lift Mr. Sage into the carriage?"

They struggled to drag, pull and lift Sage into the body of the carriage, but, with a few pauses while Susan let faintness and nausea pass, they managed it. They left him lying on a seat. Billy had wanted to leave him on the floor of the carriage, but Susan had objected.

"I want him to be in my sight, not around my feet where he could try to do some further injury to me," she explained. "I will need the pistol while we travel."

Billy looked shocked. "Would you use it?"

"I doubt it, but while I'm in the same space as Mr. Sage, I feel I need the protection the gun offers. I doubt my face will ever be the same after his punch landed," Susan said, touching her chin gingerly.

"You've got a heck of a bruise already."

"I must look a fright, for I know I'm covered in dust from head to foot. Let's try to return to the inn we left from, for no one else would believe our Banbury story."

Susan exited the carriage. When Billy was seated, nervously, in the coachman's seat, she gave him instructions for handling the horses. They were being very docile, and she hoped that they were indeed tired and therefore more inclined to walk steadily along the type of lanes they'd already traversed.

When she was happy Billy was as confident as he ever was going to be, she climbed into the carriage and slammed the door. Relieved when she heard Billy's instruction and the carriage lurched forwards, she sat back against the seat. Every part of her ached, but she couldn't afford to be complacent.

Whenever the vehicle hit a hole in the poorly maintained lanes, both Susan and Mr. Sage were thrown around. How Billy had managed to keep himself secreted away when she'd already uttered an 'oof' on more than one occasion, she would never know.

Susan sat up straighter when she noticed Mr. Sage opening his eyes slowly. She watched, pointing the pistol at him, as he blinked and tried to focus on his surroundings. She tried to set her face into an impassive expression. She could not show any weakness, for she knew he would take advantage of it, even in his weakened state.

"Well, this is an unexpected development," Mr. Sage croaked, licking his lips in an effort to get his mouth working.

"Remain still and nothing will happen to you," Susan instructed.

"Who is driving the carriage?"

"No one of your concern."

"You're looking a little peaky. I think you should put the pistol down, and we can talk this through. I'm sure we could come to an arrangement that would suit us both," Mr. Sage said, trying to sit himself up.

"Please stay where you are."

"I'm damned uncomfortable and losing sensation in my arms – added to that I've got a banging headache, which hurts even more when my head touches the seat. Have some mercy on a man."

"You don't deserve anything after what you've done," Susan said. "But I'll allow you to sit up. Just don't try any further movement."

"Come, come, my lady. The gun isn't even primed. Don't try to convince me that you would be willing to fire at me should I try to escape," Mr. Sage taunted.

Pausing only for a second, Susan pulled back the hammer on the flintlock pistol, priming it. "I'm sure I don't need to check if it is already loaded," she said calmly. "I'm sure you wouldn't have braved a yard full of people if you weren't prepared to use your weapon. Someone might have been foolish enough to approach you."

Mr. Sage narrowed his eyes. "So, you have a little more fight in you than I presumed. I'd foolishly thought you were naught but a wittering baggage. My mistake. But not one I will make again. Just know this: I don't take having a pistol pointed at me lightly. You will suffer as a result of your impudence."

"Yet it was perfectly acceptable for you to stick the thing into my ribs," Susan snapped.

"It was a means to an end." Mr. Sage shrugged. "If you think I am going to be taken meekly to the nearest magistrate and charged with kidnap, you have underestimated me."

"Kidnap and murder. You might have forgotten what you did to Mr. Malone, but I certainly haven't."

"Ah yes, Albert. He was such a bore," Mr. Sage said conversationally. "I should thank you for reminding me

201

about that. I had forgotten for the moment. Realising my mistake convinces me even further than I have nothing to lose."

"With regard to what?" Susan's gut feeling was screaming that she should leave the carriage.

"All this." Mr. Sage looked around the carriage. "If I am caught, I shall swing for what I've done. There is nothing that can happen to save me. So the question I have to ask is what do I do with you?"

"You might be transported," Susan said, knowing that she was losing the situation but not expert enough to regain control. Her heart was pounding uncomfortably but she tried to remain outwardly calm.

"After murdering a returning war hero? And then kidnapping a titled young woman? You're a foolish chit if you think they'd do anything but make me swing. Unsurprisingly, that fate doesn't appeal to me."

"You perhaps should have thought of that before you embarked on your nefarious activities. None of this had anything to do with anything other than your own greed," Susan scolded.

"It would have been fine and dandy if that friend of yours had agreed to marry me. None of this would have happened. I hope she realises when she visits your grave that it's her fault you're dead," Mr. Sage said seriously.

"I don't under—" Susan's words were lost as Mr Sage threw himself across the carriage.

Too late, she realised he had wriggled out of his hand bindings, although he was still constrained by the ties around his feet. He grabbed the hand that was holding the pistol.

Susan struggled to keep hold of the weapon, but the carriage lurched, sending them both into the carriage wall.

As the two bodies thudded into the luxurious material, a gunshot rang out, and they fell back onto the seat they'd vacated.

Susan stared down in horror at the red stain on her dress, before looking, wide-eyed, at the stunned expression on Mr. Sage's face.

Chapter 22

"There must be a more efficient way of doing this," Miles muttered as they separated at yet another junction. Each had been travelling down the lanes and returning when finding no sign of a carriage or its occupants.

"We found where they turned off the main road," Dunn reasoned. "Nothing but a large carriage could have caused that amount of damage to the bushes."

"And we've found other evidence. We're only checking every lane to make doubly sure," Jones added.

"You must be really worried," Miles said. "When you're being reassuring, I know it's time to be concerned."

"Not at all. I have a score to settle with Sage, if it is him," Jones said. "I am very keen to reacquaint myself with him and shall search until there are no horses left to carry me."

Dunn and Miles exchanged a look but said nothing.

"These lanes are a nightmare to traverse down. It's about time some of these holes were filled. They're a damned nuisance," Jones said, sounding more like his usual laconic self.

"I can see the powers that be filling in holes just for your convenience," Dunn said dryly.

"They've nothing better to do from what I can see," Jones replied. "There's a building there. I shall ride down and enquire if our elusive carriage was seen."

The pair left Jones behind and continued on their way. Jones would catch them up, so there was no point in their wasting time by waiting for him.

"He's itching for a fight," Dunn said.

"Yes. He can have one," Miles responded darkly. "I just want to make sure Susan is unharmed."

"She's a strong woman," Dunn said gently. "She bore what happened with the kidnap with fortitude."

"Yes. She's been undervalued and underestimated her whole life, I think," Miles admitted.

"I hope at least her new husband will appreciate her as she should be."

Miles shot Dunn a glance but didn't respond to the comment at first. Then his expression changed to that of anguish. "All that I keep thinking about is that she could be hurt and I never told her how I felt. She could die not knowing that I love her."

"Well halle-bloody-lujah," Dunn responded. "You've finally realised what we saw on board the ship."

"It was still wrong to place the bet."

"Yes. Probably," Dunn said. "But without it you'd never have married her and acknowledged you have feelings for her."

"Perhaps," Miles conceded. "I just wish we could find them!"

They were prevented from further conversation by the sound of hooves thumping on the ground. Jones was moving at the fastest he'd done all day, and both were encouraged that he had news.

Without stopping, Jones rode past them. "Come! They were down this way but a half hour ago. They took the next turning, which doesn't have any offshoots for miles. We're nearly on them!"

The three immediately picked up speed, no one speaking as they navigated the ruts and holes. Miles had to force himself to focus on remaining in his seat, or his thoughts of Susan would overtake his concentration. Heart pounding, he urged his horse forwards.

Dunn saw the top of the carriage as the hedges in the lane dipped and showed what lay beyond a bend. He immediately slowed, pointing without speaking at the vehicle.

"It's moving very slowly," he said when the three had come to a stop.

"We can't rush in like a herd of elephants," Miles said quickly.

"Or like a cavalryman charging at the French?" Jones asked with a grin.

"No. Definitely not like that." Miles frowned as he watched the carriage trundle along. "Billy is guiding the horses."

"The cabin boy?" Dunn asked.

"It looks like it," Miles said. "Come, let's approach carefully."

Miles led the trio along the lane. They moved faster than the carriage was moving, but not quickly enough that they would draw attention to themselves. When they were within a few hundred yards of the vehicle, Miles indicated that he would go to the right and Dunn and Jones should go to the left.

"There's no opportunity of getting Billy to stop the carriage without our arrival being noticed," he said quietly, not wishing his voice to carry, although the sound of the wheels would have been enough to drown out any noise coming from the threesome.

"It's not ideal, but nothing to do with the blaggard ever seems to be straightforward," Jones grumbled.

"I'm hoping he is resting his weapon while they are so remote. Hopefully it will give you a few seconds' advantage of surprise. I'll leave you to deal with him. I just need to get Susan away from danger," Miles said.

"Understood, Longdon," Jones said. "We'll get her out of this."

Miles nodded at the same time as the sound of a gunshot rang out. It was clear that it came from within the carriage.

Miles shouted in anguish and kicked his heels into his horse, which took off with an objecting neigh. The carriage lurched forwards as the horses took fright at the sound, and Billy looked fit to tumble. Jones and Dunn were less than a second behind Miles in their pursuit of the runaway vehicle.

Jones, risking life and limb, forced his horse to one the side of the carriage. Fast-turning wheels threatened to cripple his animal as he struggled to climb on board.

"Pull the reins!" Jones shouted to Billy, who was clinging to the coachman's seat for dear life. "Pull on the bloody reins, boy!"

The sternness of the voice stirred Billy into action. He grabbed the loose leather and pulled with all of his might. The carriage horses objected loudly, but although small for his age, Billy was strong. The vehicle started to slow down.

Jones clambered onto the seat, freeing his own horse to escape from the danger that had terrified the poor animal. Taking the reins from Billy, Jones finished the job he'd started, and the carriage came to a halt.

Miles and Dunn were on either side of the rear wheels. As soon as they realised the carriage was stopping, each leapt off their animal and, drawing their pistols, they ran to the slowing vehicle. The moment it stopped, the two men yanked open the doors and stuck their now-primed guns inside.

*

Susan clung to the strap on the inside of the carriage as it lurched forward. She so wanted to be able to help Billy, but she knew there was nothing she could do. Mr. Sage and she were locked in a horrific staring competition that pinned her to her seat.

Even when the carriage came to a halt and she was startled by the sudden flinging open of both carriage doors, she couldn't tear her gaze from Mr. Sage. He would be indelibly burned into her memory from now on.

Miles stood frozen at the carriage door, staring at Susan. A large bloodstain covered her dress at her middle. She was deathly white and still as a corpse. He jumped inside the carriage and grabbed hold of her.

"Susan! No!" he wailed, pulling her towards him and rocking her in his arms. "Don't leave me! Not now! I'm sorry! I'm so sorry!"

Dunn dragged Mr. Sage out of the carriage and instantly realised he was dead. Returning to the inside, he saw the discharged gun on the floor between the two seats.

"Miles! Miles, check her over!" Dunn shouted at his friend.

Miles looked at Dunn, who repeated the instruction. Reluctantly, he moved Susan from his arms to inspect her. He immediately noticed that her eyes had moved to follow the body of Mr. Sage, which was now lying on the ground outside the carriage. She was alive. His worst fear was wrong. She lived!

He moved his face in front of hers so she could no longer see the body. "Susan, can you hear me? Are you hurt? Did you get shot?"

Susan stared uncomprehendingly at her husband.

With a gargantuan effort, Miles pushed his inner turmoil aside and focused on his wife. She was in shock, and that could be dangerous. He held her face gently with one hand, forcing her to look into his eyes.

"Susan. Listen to me," he said quietly, but firmly. "You are safe. I'm here. Remember you said that you knew I'd come when you were kidnapped? Well, I'm here again. It looks like you can't rid yourself of me. Susan, I need to know if you are injured. There is blood on your dress. Are you hurt?"

It was like being pulled from somewhere dark and terrifying as the words sank into Susan's consciousness. Grey eyes pierced into her very soul as they stared into hers. Those beautiful grey eyes that she'd loved for so long. They were worried and anxious. She didn't like it when Miles was upset. It would give him nightmares. She had to help him, to bring a smile to his lips, or he would have a disturbed night.

Susan sighed and blinked a few times. "Miles?" she whispered.

"Oh, my darling girl. Yes, I'm here. Are you hurt? Please tell me you aren't," Miles asked gently.

"The gun," Susan said. "It went off."

"I know. I heard it," Miles said. "Are you hurt?" He was trying to resist the urge to wrap her into his arms where he could keep her safe.

"Me? I don't know."

Miles's stomach lurched at her words. Sometimes people didn't know they'd been hurt when they'd received a fatal wound. The body went into shock, removing the reality of the situation from the person's suffering.

Dunn had sat quietly throughout the exchange, but now he touched Miles's arm. "You need to check her over."

Miles nodded and felt along Susan's arms. He knew she wasn't injured there, but he wanted to check her over fully. As he felt around her waist, she gave no indication of feeling pain, so his hands moved to her stomach where the bloodstain was.

Instead of pressing on her middle, he pulled the material of her dress taut. He sagged with relief, before turning to Dunn. "There's no bullet mark."

"Thank God," Dunn said. "I thought there was only one gun, and I was sure we heard only one gunshot. It must be Sage's blood."

Susan seemed to stir herself at Dunn's words and looked down in horror at her dress. She started to moan and try to brush off the stain. "No. No. No."

Miles wrapped her in his arms, stopping her from becoming hysterical. "Shh," he soothed. "We're going to return to the inn and get you a nice warm bath. I'm here. You're safe. I promise you, you're safe." Turning to Dunn, Miles spoke quietly. "We need to move immediately."

"Understood." Dunn jumped out of the carriage and closed the door. Miles listened, at the same time whispering comforting words to Susan.

Dunn was giving instructions whilst attaching their horses to the rear of the carriage. He clambered onto the footboard that footmen usually used, leaving Jones and Billy to sit up front. None of them considered moving Mr. Sage's body from where it had landed on the ground. The only place suitable for it would have been on one of the horses, or the inside the carriage, and none of the grouping would contemplate either of those. His location would be relayed later, but for now he was left.

A fitting end for a man without conscience.

Chapter 23

It felt like hours to Miles before they arrived back at the inn. He was hoarse with speaking constantly to Susan, who had been unresponsive throughout the journey. Her lack of reaction was more worrying than if she'd had a fit of hysterics.

As soon as they entered the inn yard, Dunn jumped off the step he'd travelled on and started giving orders. Opening the carriage door, he popped his head in. "I've ordered a warm bath for Susan and the doctor to be brought. Can you carry her to her room?"

"Of course," Miles answered. "Susan, we're here, back at the inn. Come, we need to get you to your room."

The only response that Miles received was that she gripped his greatcoat when he attempted to climb down the steps. It encouraged him that at least she wanted him near her.

"I'm only stepping down so that I can carry you upstairs. Come, my darling, I'll be with you the whole time," he assured her gently.

Lifting her into his arms, Miles walked into the inn. Susan's maid, having been alerted to her mistress's return, guided Miles to the bedchamber.

"I shall take over from here, my lord," the maid said, as a regular line of staff entered the room, bringing buckets full of hot water to fill the bath.

"I'm going to care for my wife," Miles said firmly. "You go and arrange food and drink and wait for the doctor."

The maid pursed her lips. "She needs bathing and careful handling, my lord. I've known her since she was a babe, and I'm quite capable of tending to her needs."

"And I am her husband, who will be looking after her for the remainder of her days." Miles forced himself not to snap at the long-time member of staff. "I will be caring for my wife, and only I."

Muttering darkly, the maid left the room. There was little she could do with her mistress so unresponsive, but she would be having words with Susan when the time came. Husbands who picked and chose when they wanted a wife didn't rest easy with a woman intent on defending her mistress.

Miles waited until the room was empty and the bath full and steaming before he undressed Susan. She shivered at his touch but stood mutely before him. He lifted her into the water, not caring that his shirt sleeves were drenched by the action. He took the soap and washed her. Carefully and with reverence, he released her hair and tenderly washed each curl.

When he was satisfied she was warmed through, he lifted her out of the water and wrapped her in towels. Talking to her all the time, reassuring her and explaining everything he was doing, he dried her hair by the fire and then helped her to get dressed in her nightclothes. He pulled a blanket off the bed, wrapped them both in it, and sat with her on his knee on the chair closest to the fire.

A knock on the door brought the return of the maid with the doctor. Neither reacted to the strange scene of Miles wrapping himself around Susan protectively.

"Have you been told of what's happened?" Miles asked.

"Yes, my lord. I would like to examine your wife. If you could carry her to the bed," the doctor instructed.

Miles did as he was told, and although he longed to climb into the bed with Susan, he satisfied himself with sitting on the edge and holding her hand. The doctor approached Susan from the opposite side. After a few moments of examining her, he seemed satisfied, although Susan was mainly unresponsive to him.

"She's in shock because of what she's experienced. Your friend informed me of what happened," the doctor said. "You've done the right thing in keeping her warm. Leave her in bed, give her fluids, but don't worry if she doesn't wish to eat at the moment. I shall leave some laudanum for her to take. It will help her to rest through the night. I don't anticipate her reaction to be of the long-lasting kind."

"Will we be able to travel home on the morrow?" Miles asked.

"If she seems recovered, she should be fine. Just take the journey slowly, and keep her warm and calm."

"I will. Thank you."

The doctor nodded his goodbye and left the room. Miles waited until the maid returned, as he knew she would.

"I'm staying here tonight," he said as soon as she entered the room. "Arrange for some food to be brought, and I'll eat when Lady Longdon is asleep. Expect to return to London tomorrow. In the meantime, please allow Captains Jones and Dunn entry. I need to speak to them for a moment."

The maid did as requested, and it wasn't long before the two friends filled the doorway, their eyes full of concern for Susan.

"What do you need from us?" Dunn asked.

"I just want to thank you for today. Having you with me was a great help," Miles said. "Although trying to get yourself killed was not part of the plan." He smiled at the memory of Jones squeezing himself into the tiny space between the carriage and the hedge.

"We had to stop the carriage. Billy wasn't experienced enough," Jones said with a nonchalant shrug.

"How is the boy?" Miles asked, having forgotten about the lad.

"Halfway between shocked and thrilled at having an adventure and surviving it. He's been pacing the tap room below, worried about his mistress, though," Dunn supplied.

"She'll be fine, especially when I get her home." Miles glanced at his wife. She was lying with her eyes closed, but he knew by the pressure on his hand that she was awake.

"Are you going to Barrowfoot tomorrow?" Dunn asked.

"No. We're closer to London, so I'll return there. I don't want to remain in this inn any longer than I have to. Fresh memories are needed to replace the horror," Miles said with authority.

"She'll recover," Jones said.

"I hope so."

"We will escort you back. I know there is no further threat, but we'll both be happier to know we've delivered you to Curzon Street," Dunn said.

"Thank you. I would appreciate it," Miles replied.

When he was left alone with Susan, he supported her in order that she could drink the laudanum. She'd looked at him in question when he'd said she should drink it.

"Tonight you need a dreamless sleep," he said gently, kissing the top of her head. "I won't leave you for a moment."

"Will the sight of him ever go away?" Susan asked in a whisper.

"Not completely," Miles answered honestly. "But we'll make sure it is only there in the background. You'll be able to live with that. I promise."

Susan nodded slightly and closed her eyes, letting the medication take its effect. It wasn't long before she was breathing deeply and was finally relaxed.

Miles moved to where the table was laden with food. It was a few moments before he could swallow anything, her absolute faith in him causing a lump in his throat and stinging behind his eyes.

When he had control of himself, he ate a few mouthfuls and then undressed quickly. He climbed into bed with Susan and gently pulled her towards him.

"You might be in a deep sleep," he whispered into her ear. "But know that I'm here should you need me. I'm right next to you, my love."

*

Susan looked out of the window as the damaged carriage made its way back to London. She would owe her aunt a refurbished vehicle body, as it was covered in scratches and marks from its rough treatment the previous day.

Miles was sitting next to her, holding her hand as they moved along at a fast pace. Her maid and Billy were seated opposite them. She took comfort in Miles's presence and contact but worried about what would happen when they returned to London. They would be forced to have a difficult conversation, which couldn't take place in a carriage with servants, but as far as she could see, their situation hadn't changed. Miles had regretted marrying her, and she had a broken heart, and now she was struggling with the image of the man she had shot.

She'd asked Miles about the consequences as he'd helped her to dress. It directed her thoughts to somewhere other than the fact her husband was dressing her.

"I've killed a man. Will I hang?" she asked in a whisper.

Miles paused. "No. Not at all. I know Jones and Dunn have taken care of everything with the magistrate. There will be no charges."

"But he's dead, and it was I who fired the gun."

"We can't be sure of that fact," Miles said. "There was a struggle, and the gun went off. You can't be completely certain it was you who pulled the trigger. But even if you could, he'd abducted you and held you at gunpoint, for the second time. There wouldn't be any charges against you in whichever circumstances." He kissed his wife gently. "It's over, Susan. There is nothing to worry about anymore."

Susan stopped herself from arguing against him. She had a lot to worry about. Where she was going to live. What she was going to do, and how the devil she would be able to live without the man who had rescued her for a second time. Resting her head against the seat of the carriage, she blindly looked out of the window.

217

Chapter 24

When they arrived back in Curzon Street, Miles insisted that Susan go immediately to her bedchamber and rest. He watched her being taken upstairs by her maid with a frown on his face. His wife had never been so unresponsive and withdrawn. It increased his worry about her.

He thanked his friends, who insisted they would return to their own lodgings without delay. As they asked to be kept informed about Susan's recovery, Miles shook their hands.

"Thank you, again," he said.

"It was a drastic way to overcome the consequences of our misguided interference, but I'm glad we're on speaking terms once more," Dunn said, shaking his friend's hand.

"He'd have soon found he couldn't live without us." Jones slapped Miles on the back. "Look after that wife of yours. She's precious to us."

"And to me," Miles admitted.

After seeing his friends out, he went to his study. He sent a missive to Ralph and Edith and one to Aunt Florence, updating them briefly on what had happened but instructing them all that he wouldn't allow any visitors that day. He then went in to see his mother.

She was seated in the drawing room with her two companions and looked up in surprise at her son's entrance.

"Mother, I've returned with Susan, who isn't well at the moment," Miles said, brushing over everything that had gone between them the last few days.

"Is she sickening for something?"

"I think so, and I think it might be contagious," Miles said quickly. "I'm concerned for your well-being. I wouldn't like to see you come down with the same malaise."

If the son had wished to cause consternation with his mother, he couldn't have chosen a better subject. Her natural hypochondria came immediately to the fore.

"Oh, my dear me. What are we to do? I can't risk catching anything. I've been in such poor health recently, I would surely take a turn for the worse if I were to come down with anything else."

"I was thinking perhaps a trip to Brighton? Only at the best address, of course," Miles said smoothly.

"That's a good idea. I could watch the sea bathers," his mother replied. "I'd be out of harm's way. Yes. We should do that. So considerate of you, Miles. I shall prepare to leave tomorrow."

"I have already sent an express to arrange accommodation," Miles said.

"I have such a thoughtful son," she said to her nodding companions.

Miles bowed, and left the room with a smile on his face. He was a selfish son, but he had no remorse. He had to convince his wife that he cared for her, and having his mother close by would only hinder his progress.

His next instruction was to his staff. "Lady Longdon and myself are not at home to visitors. There will no doubt be a visit from my sister, and she can come in, or she'll just set up camp outside, but no one else. And I mean no one."

"Of course, my lord," the butler replied.

Miles returned to his sitting room, expecting to see Susan, but it was empty. He knocked on his wife's door and opened it. Entering, he was surprised to see Susan in bed.

Her maid approached him. "She claimed exhaustion, my lord," the maid whispered. "Said she wanted nothing but to sleep. Might be the after-effects of the laudanum."

"Perhaps," Miles said, his eyes never leaving his wife. "I shall remain next door. Call me the moment she awakens."

"Yes, my lord."

*

Miles awoke with a start. It was dark, the fire had died in the grate, and he was damned stiff and uncomfortable. He stretched, presuming that his position had become uncomfortable enough to waken him, but then he heard a sound coming from Susan's chamber.

He was at her door in two strides, all stiffness and discomfort forgotten. Opening the door, he saw Susan was alone and thrashing around in her bed.

Immediately he went to his wife and lifted her into his arms. "Susan, I'm here. You're safe," Miles soothed.

Susan had stilled at his moving her, but she started to beat him with her fists, trying to escape. "No. No. Let me go!" she wailed.

At first Miles thought she was rejecting him, but he soon realised that she was still in the middle of her terrors. Holding her tightly, he continued to speak calmly and reassuringly, his heart aching that she was suffering so.

Eventually, his words seemed to calm her. He felt the change in her even before she grabbed hold of his waistcoat with both hands and started to cry into his chest.

It was a relief for Miles to see the release. Her containment of her feelings wasn't healthy, but now, through tears, she would hopefully start to recover from the events she'd experienced.

"It's over, Susan. You're here with me, and I won't let anything happen to you again."

Susan looked up at her husband, her cheeks wet with tears and eyes red. "I can't let you waste your life on me. I don't make you happy. You should be free to make your own choice, as you wanted."

"I don't understand," Miles said. "Please explain why I would want to do that."

"You told me you wanted to have been able to choose your own wife," Susan sobbed. "I can't stay with you, Miles. My conscience won't let me. Nothing else matters. You've given me so much. I can't make you suffer any longer."

"The night I was drunk," Miles said dully.

"They say you speak the truth when you are drunk." Susan hiccupped, gaining control of herself and trying to pull away from Miles. She hated herself for always wishing to turn to him, but she supposed that was what happened when you were in love with someone.

"Susan, I wasn't angry at you. I was in a temper with Jones and Dunn and that blasted bet," Miles said.

"It amounts to the same thing." Susan reached for a handkerchief and blew her nose. "The bet caused your marriage, and now you are trapped. I don't condemn you. It's mainly down to my stepmother, but I refuse to make you live with the consequences of her malice."

"I am going to send your stepmother the biggest bouquet of flowers I can buy. In fact, I might send her three," Miles said with a smile.

221

"Why would you do that?"

"I'm a nodcock for behaving the way I did, and I beg your forgiveness, but I need to say something before I go on my knees and beg mercy."

"I think you must be a little out of sorts. You aren't making sense."

"I was wallowing in self-pity, but I hadn't seen what everyone else had," Miles said gently. "I love you, Susan."

If Miles had expected Susan to melt into his arms at his words, he was to be disappointed. She pulled away from him so violently that he hadn't time to react. She crawled to the opposite side of the bed and sat there, shaking her head at him.

"What have I said that is so repulsive?" Miles said, half amused, half astounded.

"Don't lie to me," Susan answered sharply. "I can cope with knowing you like me but nothing else, but if you try to deceive me, I couldn't bear it. Please don't say words we both know you don't mean."

"Susan, my sweetheart, I'm not lying." Miles smiled. "I promise on my honour, I'm not."

Putting her head in her hands, Susan moaned. Miles took the opportunity to move towards her.

"Come here, you foolish girl," he said, wrapping his arms around her. "Let me explain something to you. Will you listen? Really listen?"

"Yes, but I can't promise to believe you."

"You really have spent too much time with my sister," Miles said with a chuckle. "When we were aboard the *Dolphin*, apparently I couldn't take my eyes off you."

"You were concerned about me," Susan interrupted.

"Yes, I was, but it was more than that," Miles admitted for the first time. "At first I felt responsible for you,

222

because what you'd been going through was due, in part, to me. I didn't even notice the change in myself. It was only when Dunn pointed out how I'd followed your every movement with my eyes that I started to consider what had happened."

"You are an honourable man. I know you are saying this out of obligation."

"I hadn't realised until this moment that I'd married a harpy." Miles kissed Susan gently. He stroked where she'd been punched, a fleeting look of anger crossing his expression as he thought of someone hurting her. "Will you let me continue? I always thought you were dissimilar to Edith, but I'm coming to realise you have similarities in refusing to listen when I have something important to say."

Susan gave him a look but nodded.

"Good. When we returned, neither of us enjoyed the speculation around our marriage. We aren't like Jones, who enjoys being the centre of attention, I think we both tend to remain in the background if we can," Miles said. "When I awoke from my drunken stupor and one of the worst nightmares I'd had in a long time, I began to really understand myself."

"You suffered a nightmare?" Susan asked in alarm.

"Yes. And I deserved it to be horrendous," Miles said. "You weren't there with me. I realised that your presence soothes me, makes me happier, which, although it might not have been a benefit of getting married that I'd imagined, I can't say I'm sorry about."

Susan frowned, and Miles kissed her again. "Wait," he said. "I knew I needed to reach you and make amends. For I understand you enough to know you wouldn't have left me lightly. Dunn and Jones happened to call and insisted on accompanying me because they think a lot of you and felt that they had something to apologise for. I'm now so glad they came along. When we reached the inn and found out what had happened, I honestly thought I was going to collapse. The thought of you in danger again sent my blood cold, and for a moment I was unable to think, let alone act."

"I think Mr. Sage started to regret choosing me. He said I annoyed him to the devil," Susan said.

Miles once more touched the bruise on her chin. "If he'd been alive when we reached you, I'd have killed him for inflicting this on you," he said, his anger barely contained. "We were approaching the carriage when the gunshot went off. But I'd just admitted something to Dunn."

"Oh?"

"I'd admitted that you'd left me and were in danger, and I was distraught because I'd never told you how much I love you," Miles said. "I don't deserve your love, because I've behaved abominably, but believe me, the worst moment of my entire life was when I opened that carriage door and saw blood on your dress. If I'd lost you then, I think I'd have put my own pistol to my head and pulled the trigger."

Susan winced. "Don't say that!"

"It was how I felt," Miles said. "In all the battles I've taken part in, all the friends I've lost, all the bloodshed I've seen, I have never been affected in such a way. I thought I'd lost you, and I couldn't stand it. I knew I loved you before I reached the carriage. The events after opening that door only proved to me that I hadn't realised just how much."

Susan remained silent when Miles had stopped speaking. Miles watched her closely, his eyes unsure and a little wary.

"Am I too late? Are you so repulsed by my actions that it's spoiled what feelings you had for me?" he asked quietly when it seemed Susan wasn't going to speak.

Susan was in turmoil. If she could have believed his words, he would have just made her the happiest woman alive, but there was doubt in her mind.

"You are known so well for being honourable," she said in answer. "I can't let this be one of those occasions."

"It isn't. I swear on everything that is precious to me," Miles insisted. "Let me prove it to you. Let's get married again, a huge wedding, showing the whole of London that I love you dearly."

"We can't do that."

"With you by my side, I feel I can do anything," Miles said. "You are the first person I have ever wanted to spend the night with. You know everything about me, even my demons, and you don't ridicule me for them. You are the first thing I think of in the morning, and the last thing I think of at night and, if my valet is to be believed, the person I called out for most during the night you were away from me."

Susan covered her blushing cheeks with her hands. "What must he think of us?"

"I'd like to hope he thinks we are a couple who are deeply in love," Miles said. "Can you love me again, Susan? Or do I have to love us enough for the both of us?"

"I thought that I could do that once, but it's impossible. No matter how hard you try, when only one person loves it isn't enough."

"I promise I'll do everything I can to make this work. I want you by my side. I need you with me. Can you forgive me? Even if there is the slightest chance you could forgive

225

me in the next ten years, I'll take those odds. I will have something to work on."

"I forgave you the morning after your drunken words," Susan said. "There is nothing to forgive." She touched Miles's face gently, boldened by what she'd heard.

"I would have made me pay with jewels at least," Miles said with a smile. "What about the love part? Is there a little bit of you that still cares for me?"

"I couldn't stop loving you if I tried," Susan admitted.

Miles sighed. "That is music to my ears."

"I'm afraid to believe you, though," she said. "It's such a change."

"It doesn't matter that you doubt me. That I can deal with. I will prove to you with every breath I take that we were meant to be together. At least I know I've not completely ruined our marriage," Miles said. "I'm going to consider that today is our anniversary day, for this is the day we were honest with each other, and it's the start of our future life together."

"It's the middle of the night," Susan pointed out.

"Nights are a perfect time to be alone enough to enjoy each other's company, don't you think?" Miles said, standing.

Susan's heart started to pound. "I-I suppose so."

"Good. I hope you don't expect much sleep tonight, Lady Longdon. I have some making up to do," Miles said, stripping off his waistcoat. "And I think I know the perfect way to start." He smiled as Susan opened her arms to him. "Oh, I do love you," he said quietly, climbing into bed to be enfolded by her embrace.

Epilogue

Anyone hearing the rumour of the shaky start to married life that Lord and Lady Longdon had experienced might suspect it was a sham of a marriage. Being in their company for half an hour would put to rest any suspicion that such was the case. In fact, there was more scandal attached to the couple because of the besotted behaviour of Lord Longdon towards his wife than there was about their wedding.

Miles and Susan never spent a day apart after they had admitted their love to each other. If Miles had business, he would insist Susan travel with him. When Susan was increasing and beyond the time of safe travel, Miles would remain at his wife's side.

Mrs. King took the credit for her daughter's fortuitous marriage, which the couple never disputed. They rarely saw the woman, so she had no impact on their happiness. Mr. King would often visit his daughter, claiming he was checking his son-in-law didn't need any financial advice, but in reality was always to be found in the nursery playing with his grandchildren.

Edith, Ralph and Aunt Florence were the family who meant the most to the couple, sharing life events and travelling between the houses. Edith adopted Aunt Florence as her own relative, and the five of them were often together.

Susan and Miles had eleven children: five boys and six girls. Susan loved that all of her children had the grey eyes of their father.

Miles's nightmares never really disappeared, although they reduced and weren't as debilitating when they struck. Susan and Ashurst the valet had perfected the process of soothing the terrors. Susan understood what her husband was going through even more having experienced her own for the first few months after her kidnap. Miles was there for her during those nights, just as she was when he needed her.

Billy settled into life at Barrowfoot House. He became a footman but was a special favourite with the children and was very often allowed to accompany the nanny on excursions. On those occasions he spent more time on his knees, having eleven adoring small people climbing all over him.

Miles's mother settled in Brighton, and although she visited her son and daughter occasionally, she kept those visits to a minimum. Children very often had illnesses, and it didn't suit her constitution, which she claimed was fragile until she eventually died in her eightieth year.

Jones and Dunn were always welcome visitors to the Longdon household. They took it upon themselves to ensure that each honorary niece or nephew was a proficient horseman or woman, much to the disgust of the grooms employed for the job. They would eventually settle down themselves, but they had to have adventures of their own first ... but that's another story. (Captain Jones's Temptation)

The End

About this book

When I started *Lady Edith's Lonely Heart*, it was going to be a standalone novel. I had wanted to write it for a long time and hadn't thought beyond writing Edith's story.

Then Miles and Susan started to develop characters with stories to tell of their own.

Kidnapping and ransom of heiresses was quite common in Regency times. If the men weren't of the same class and therefore wouldn't have the chance to compromise the heiress, they often resorted to more nefarious methods. The unfortunate girls had money, but it didn't mean they were safe or happy; very often they were an afterthought. The money was the main focus of everyone's attention.

This story was going to be the second part of a two-part story, but then Jones and Dunn came along …

Captain Jones's Temptation – available 3rd September 2020!

About the Author

I have had the fortune to live a dream. I've always wanted to write, but life got in the way as it so often does until a few years ago. Then a change in circumstance enabled me to do what I loved: sit down to write. Now writing has taken over my life, holidays being based around research, so much so that no matter where we go, my long-suffering husband says, 'And what connection to the Regency period has this building/town/garden got?'

That dream became a little more surreal when in 2018, I became an Amazon StorytellerUK Finalist with Lord Livesey's Bluestocking. A Regency Romance in the top five of an all-genre competition! It was a truly wonderful experience, I didn't expect to win, but I had a ball at the awards ceremony.

I do appreciate it when readers get in touch, especially if they love the characters as much as I do. Those first few weeks after release is a trying time; I desperately want everyone to love my characters that take months and months of work to bring to life.

If you enjoy the books please would you take the time to write a review on Amazon? Reviews are vital for an author who is just starting out, although I admit to bad ones being crushing. Selfishly I want readers to love my stories!

I can be contacted for any comments you may have, via my website:

www.audreyharrison.co.uk

or

www.facebook.com/AudreyHarrisonAuthor

Please sign-up for email/newsletter – only sent out when there is something to say!

www.audreyharrison.co.uk

You'll receive a free copy of The Unwilling Earl in mobi format for signing-up as a thank you!

Novels by Audrey Harrison

Regency Romances – newest release first

Lady Edith's Lonely Heart

Miss King's Rescue

The Lonely Lord

The Drummond Series:-

Lady Lou the Highwayman – Drummond series Book 1

Saving Captain Drummond – Drummond Series Book 2

Lord Livesey's Bluestocking (Amazon Storyteller Finalist 2018)

Return to the Regency – A Regency Time-travel novel

My Foundlings:-

The Foundling Duke – The Foundlings Book 1

The Foundling Lady – The Foundlings Book 2

Book bundle – **The Foundlings**

Mr Bailey's Lady

The Spy Series:-

My Lord the Spy

My Earl the Spy

Book bundle – **The Spying Lords**

The Captain's Wallflower

Other Eras

A Very Modern Lord

Years Apart

Printed in Poland
by Amazon Fulfillment
Poland Sp. z o.o., Wrocław